T0208852

THE
UNEXPECTED
WAR

A NEW BEGINNING

JEAN-PIERRE BRETON

THE
UNEXPECTED
WAR

A NEW BEGINNING

THE UNEXPECTED WAR
A NEW BEGINNING

This is a work of fiction. All of the characters, names, incidents, organizations, and dialogue in this novel are either the products of the author's imagination or are used fictitiously.

iUniverse books may be ordered through booksellers or by contacting:

iUniverse
1663 Liberty Drive
Bloomington, IN 47403
www.iuniverse.com
1-800-Authors (1-800-288-4677)

ISBN: 978-1-4917-7709-1 (sc)
ISBN: 978-1-4917-7708-4 (e)

Library of Congress Control Number: 2015953733

Print information available on the last page.

iUniverse rev. date: 10/5/2015

CHAPTER 1

It's funny when you look at how every action in life has a reaction. I was a simple kid with simple problems. I never wanted this, any of it—the role of a leader, father, husband, and hero to mankind. If you had asked me then where I would be when I grew up, I would have told you probably lying on a buddy's floor drinking a cold beer.

Then the war happened. It has been five years since the fiends invaded Earth in search of a new home. Their own planet of Fraturna had been waged in an unwinnable war against the Relicks years prior.

Not all of them wanted war, but we humans fear things we cannot control, and when the fiends struck, we struck back. Like I said, every action has a reaction. Now, five years later, millions of lives both fiend and human have been lost in a war that has no end in sight.

When I had been taken prisoner by the fiends, I thought I would succumb to the same fate as the others. That was not the case though. I met Lara, a fiend who seemed genuinely compassionate about my well-being. She helped me survive that hellhole where we had forged our love for each other, a feeling I thought I would never feel again after Rachel had been killed in a fiend's assault on our village.

Lara and I eventually had a child together, naming her Rashellia in Rachel's honor. We had coined the term half-blood to describe a creature that was half human, half fiend. She was the first half-blood the world had ever seen and had extraordinary powers that one could never begin to imagine.

So many lives had been lost for her protection—first Tracy's, then my best friend David's, my sister Tina's, and now mine. The fiends took her from Lara and me in an ambush on the city of Monatello to be a guinea pig in some lab for the rest of her life.

I died on that beach the night of the assault on Monatello in the arms of Lara, the only one left who truly cared for me—or at least that's what I had thought, anyway. The dull flicker of a candle against the rocky surface of an underwater cavern was the only source of light as I gasped in a breath, feeling the unfamiliar, stale air course through my lungs.

My chest pounded, and I felt as though my heart was going to explode. "Shh, shh, Lance. It's okay," the gentle voice of a female soothed me as I slowly came to my senses.

I felt the soft touch against my skin as she tried to relax my confused, panicked expression while everything began to come into focus. "Lara? … This is impossible," I whispered.

"I'm dead … This is impossible," I repeated, glancing around the underwater cavern that held us prisoner.

Lara leaned down and placed a kiss on my cheek. "You're alive, Lance," she said, a joyful tear rolling down her own cheek.

"How?" I whispered, confused, wiping the tear away from her face.

She beamed down affectionately, took my hand, and placed it against her heart. I felt the strong beating of it, my eyes widening. "You're mortal?"

She nodded. "Just like you now, Lance."

"But—"

Lara held up her hand, cutting me off. "You died on that beach, but I gave up my immortality in return for your life. A small price for Fiona here to resurrect you," she said, nodding to the shy Shellian in the background.

I glanced over at Fiona, who bowed her head toward me in support of Lara's story. "Rashellia?" I asked, but Lara just shook her head, avoiding my stare.

"They got her, Lance."

Her words sent a surge of anger that pulsed through my veins. Slamming my fist against the stone table, I cursed under my breath promising, "We will get her back."

Lara nodded her agreement, knowing we both would stop at nothing to achieve the final goal of having our daughter back in our arms. "Where is everyone?" I grunted in pain as I attempted to sit up.

"Relax, Lance. Everything is under control. You need your rest," she whispered, placing her hand on my chest and then laying me back down on the bed of seaweed.

Fiona vanished out of sight, reappeared a moment later with a shell filled with some kind of purplish liquid, and fed its contents to me. The medicine instantly took effect as I felt myself drifting off into unconsciousness, Lara's firm grip holding on to my hand. "I love you, Lance," she whispered and then vanished out of sight, leaving me to my dreams.

CHAPTER 2

A few weeks passed by, each day feeling more and more like a life sentence. Fiona did her best to entertain me when she was around, but lately she was always mysteriously absent. Having lain on my stone and seaweed bed for a few hours, staring at the ceiling in boredom, I got up and walked over to the edge of the cliff where the water had been pushed out by one of her spells, forming a glass-like barrier between myself and the ocean.

The village below was filled with life as Shellian citizens went about their normal day-to-day activities. The sight of the medium-sized creatures freely roaming around the ocean floor was something I was sure I would never get used to. They had invaded Earth years prior, following the fiends in search of a new planet to call home.

They slightly resembled humans but had webbed feet, ears, and hands, as well as pointy noses. The only goal the Shellians had in common with us was to witness the defeat of every last hostile fiend.

Sea life would swim by nonchalantly with some collecting rocks, others building weapons, and some sitting by their homes with food for sale. A few children were playing catch with rocks. A passing guard caught one and tossed it back to the next child.

It was such a peaceful place. I envied them in a way, knowing just above the surface the war against the fiends was still raging on. It was weird to know that a world like this existed completely oblivious to the dangers above.

My heart skipped a few beats as the eight-foot-long eel-looking dragon made its way toward the village. I knew it was Fiona, but the frightening sight of the massive creature was enough to stop any man's heart. She landed just outside the village before she took on her Shellian form.

The two guards at the entrance took a knee as she passed by. Her presence was instantly known in the village, as they played a trumpet-like instrument I had never seen before when she entered. The Shellian children all flocked around, pestering her with greetings and questions.

She spent a bit of time playing with them before glancing up at the cave I was taking shelter in. Our eyes met for a moment. She sent me a warm smile, waved her good-byes to the children, and came up to meet me at the entrance of the cave. "Greetings, Lance," she called, entering the cave through the water barrier as if it were nothing.

We took a seat at the stone table before I asked, "What's up?"

She shrugged. "Had another uneventful meeting with my father," she replied.

"How is Lord Olaf, king of the Atlantic Ocean, doing?" I asked, making sure she could catch the sarcasm in my voice.

A smile spread across her face as she seemed to hold back her laughter. "Same as always, fearful that the world is plotting against him, and so on so forth."

Reading her body language, I could tell that something was on her mind as she tapped her webbed fingers against the stone table and bit her bottom lip in thought. "What is it?" I asked.

"Huh?" she asked, looking up from the table as if she'd been torn out of a trance.

"I can tell something's on your mind, Fiona."

She shook her head. "It's no big deal. It's just that ... well ..." Her voice trailed off as she bit her bottom lip again nervously. "My father wants to meet you tomorrow. It's not very often that we have an Earth dweller living among our people for an extended amount of time."

Letting out a sigh, I nodded my agreement to meet her father. Surely this meeting was going to be more than an introduction. After all, in his eyes, I was a prisoner who had trespassed on his territory.

"Any advice?"

She shrugged. "Just follow my lead. Also never meet his eyes. It is a sign of disrespect in my culture."

I nodded my thanks, and she returned the nod. "I've caught us supper," she said in her best attempt to change the conversation.

"Right on," I muttered.

She whispered something and then ran her hand along the rocky surface of the cave. A green slime marked the path her fingers took. She then snapped her fingers, and a single spark fell from her fingers, igniting the fire. "I sure do hope its fish for supper," I said, trying to lighten the mood.

A smile spread across her face. "Today's your lucky day, then, Lance."

I laughed in mock enthusiasm. Fiona set down a small sack slung over her shoulder pulling out a few mackerels.

She sliced, gutted, and then threw them over the fire to cook. We ate in silence before going to bed. My mind was too preoccupied with the inevitable meeting with her father to focus on a conversation.

She gave me a shake the next morning, but it wasn't necessary. I hadn't slept a wink all night.

"Nervous?" she asked as I waited for her at the foot of the cave.

I shrugged. "Just want to get it over with."

"Well, then let's go, slow poke," she said and gave me a kiss.

I sent her a halfhearted smile, feeling the air around us becoming hard to breath as the power of her kiss began to take effect. "Shalanow" she whispered in her foreign tongue releasing the caves barrier.

The wall of ocean outside came smashing through the invisible barrier into the den, filling it with water. We swam out, the ocean water making it easy to breathe again. I could feel the stares of the villagers as Fiona led me to the main entrance. "Fiona, Fiona taniro!" one of the Shellian kids said to her.

We stopped as the young girl caught up to us, with a wave of Shellian children behind her. She asked Fiona something while the children stared at me in interest. Fiona laughed, glancing from the young girl to me.

"They wish to feel your skin," Fiona said.

Sharing the laugh, I took off my shirt as the children gathered around. The clammy soft feel of their webbed fingers felt odd on my skin as they ran their hands across my body. They seemed to be enjoying it though, probably never having seen a human before. The young girl who had stopped Fiona held her hand out to me. I opened mine, comparing it to hers.

A smile spread across her face as she flicked her long silver-white hair away from her face. Fiona stood off to the side, arms crossed and laughing as the children continued to play with me. The fun was soon ended though, as an angry mother came storming from the hut toward us. "Drakilo!" she yelled to her son.

The young Shellian gulped and then obediently ran over to his mother, who ordered him into their hut. She and Fiona exchanged a few heated words. Guards soon came, grabbed the woman by her arms, and dragged her into a mud hut. "Our stay here is no longer welcome, Lance," Fiona told me, motioning to finish with the kids.

I waved good-bye to them and then followed Fiona to the main entrance. The hike to her father's empire was about three hours long. As we crested the hill, the city that began to come into sight was like nothing I had ever seen before.

Palaces, made of brick, gold, and silver, lined the area below. Statues of Lord Olaf stood at every street corner. The Shellian army was actively training in the city's center while normal Shellian citizens carried on with their everyday lives.

As we neared Fiona's father's castle, three bound Shellians were dragged from a building off to our side out into the street in front of us. Six armed guards surrounded them. One was calling out a speech, probably saying what they were charged with, as a crowd gathered around the criminals. He finished his speech, and one of the armed guards pulled out a machete.

The dazzling glimmer of the blade indicated it had been sharpened in preparation for this day. The crowed began chanting something in their language. "Let's go," Fiona whispered.

I reluctantly did glance back though. The guard brought the machete down to the neck of one of the prisoners and sliced into it. The sharp cry of agony that followed was sickening.

Fiona glanced back as well. The guard decapitated the Shellian prisoner and held his head up as a triumphant roar erupted from the crowd. The body of the prisoner fell to the ground like a sack of potatoes and was kicked mercilessly by one of the guards.

"What the hell is wrong with you people?" I muttered to Fiona. "Not even the fiends are this barbaric."

"Watch your mouth, Lance," she muttered in defense to her race, but I could tell from the look on her face that she didn't agree with it either.

"Who were those people?" I asked.

"The prisoners?"

I nodded. "Nordics," she said.

"Who are they?"

"There is no time to explain. My father's place is right ahead," she told me.

The massive palace soon came into view, huge pillars of gold and stone holding it up. The two of us climbed a massive set of stairs coming to a stop at the entrance. The two Shellians standing guard took a knee at the sight of Fiona.

She motioned them up, and they asked her something. When she answered, one of them blew a horn, and the thirty-foot door of pure steel began to open. "Stay close to me," she whispered before leading me into the palace.

As we approached a throne surrounded by twenty guards, Lord Olaf came into view. "Agh, at last there is my daughter. Late as always," his gruff voice called to her.

She took a knee, bowing her head, and so did I. "Apologies, Father," she told him.

He got up and walked over to us, the long red-and-white robe trailing in his wake. "Rise, my dear," he said with a wave of his hand.

Fiona got up obediently, giving her father a cordial bow. "All is well in the eastern province of Panow," she informed him.

"Always good to hear," he said, opening his arms.

The two embraced, placing a kiss on each other's cheek. From what I could tell, the Shellians followed a very strict sequence for greetings. "This is the boy?" he asked.

"Yes, Father."

"Rise," he ordered me.

So I did. A moment of silence followed as he seemed to be sizing me up. I dared not look up, remembering that eye contact would mean nothing more than a confrontation. "What is this Earth dweller's name?" he asked Fiona.

"I can speak for myself, sir," I muttered, straightening up.

"Lance!" Fiona whispered urgently, trying to defuse the situation.

I felt her hand against my chest, holding me back, as two of the armed guards came toward us with raised spears.

Her father raised his hand, halting the guards. His attention then shifted to me. "Quite a mouth on this one," he grunted.

"Apologies, Father. He is not accustomed to our ways," Fiona explained with another cordial bow.

He laughed to himself. "Humans are all the same—disrespectful creatures that should be exterminated. I do not know nor will I understand the reason for my daughter saving your life, but I do know that you are not welcome here."

"Dad, please stop. Lance is my friend and a guest to our land," Fiona objected.

Fiona's father held his hand up to silence her before speaking again. "As much as I despise the human race, I have a pure hatred for the fiends. I have called you here today to offer you a chance to work for us, and upon your departure from our land, we will need a spy to inform us of the fiends' activities. Could we rely on you and your peers to relay that information to us?"

I couldn't help but smirk about the unbelievable arrogance of Fiona's father. "I would never work for you."

A hushed wave of murmurs from those around us instantly sprang to life as the tension grew thick in the air. Clearly no one had stood up to Lord Olaf before. I took a knee, bowed my head to him respectfully, and wished him a good day.

I turned and strode away as fast as I could. If they were going to kill me, I didn't want to see it. "Archers ready!" came the word of command from a guard.

I felt my insides tighten up as the butterflies took over, realizing this would probably be the last moment of my life, while the frantic pleas of Fiona played behind me. "Let him go," her father told the guard.

I glanced back to see him whisper something to his daughters, who gripped his arm in gratitude. She nodded, placed a kiss on his cheek, and jogged to my side. "What were you thinking, Lance. No one says no to my father," she said in a hushed whisper as we left the palace, navigating our way through the crowds of Shellians to the outskirts of the city.

"It's about time someone did, then."

She grunted her disapproval, but we continued to walk

to the outskirts. Once we were out of sight, Fiona wrapped her webbed hand around my arm, forcing me to stop. "Don't think of it as helping him, Lance. Think of it as helping me," she said in her best attempt to persuade me.

I chuckled to myself. "Nice try, Fiona." was all I could say before continuing the journey back to her village.

CHAPTER 3

"**S**o you're finally going back to the surface!" Fiona congratulated me as we sat there eating lunch.

"Finally," I agreed.

She giggled to herself. "What do you plan on doing once you're up there?"

"No clue. It's going to be like being reborn."

She gave me an understanding nod, her attention shifting back to her plate of food. Weeks had folded into months as I traveled up the long road to recovery, but finally, four months later, I was ready to get back into the war and reclaim what was mine. The two of us finished supper in silence.

"Ready?" Fiona said to me, grabbing her bow and arrows.

"As ready as I'll ever be," I responded, shouldering the backpack Lara had left behind for me.

She came over and gave me a kiss, the air of the cave instantly becoming harder to breath as her powers took over. I followed her out of the cavern into the vast rocky terrain of the ocean floor. It all felt surreal as the sand sifted through my toes, which were navigating themselves over the rocky cliff, leading down to the Shellians' village below.

With one final glance back at the underwater cave I had called home for the last four months, I quickly turned around to keep pace in Fiona's wake. "My lady," two of the village guards said, both taking a knee as we passed.

"At ease," she whispered to them with a friendly nod of her head.

"I don't think I could ever get used to that," I muttered, passing by them up a sandy trail toward a reef.

"Huh?" she asked, offering me her hand as we climbed the reef and navigated into an open field.

"If I were part of a royal family, I could never have people worship me like that," I responded.

She gave me a nonchalant shrug. "You get used to it after a while."

I laughed. "Suppose so," I grunted. "Would you like me to refer to you as 'My lady' or 'Princess Fiona' from now on?"

"Knock it off. We are friends, Lance," she called back to me, a smile spreading across her face.

"Yes, my lady," I grunted.

She laughed, giving me a playful push. I was about to return it but was stopped by the unexpected sound of agonized cries in the distance. Fiona raised her hand to me, motioning to take cover.

I did so obediently, lying down in the comfort of the wavy weeds. She drew her bow and gave me a nod of her head. I followed her, creeping along the open valley to the rocky surface of a cliff.

We were both greeted by the sight of a Shellian army below. "Your father's army?" I asked, watching as they dragged a few bound Shellians over to a rock and decapitated them with hunting knives.

"No," she explained, sadness written across her face by the sight of their murders. "Those are the Nordics. When we arrived here on Earth, some of us wanted to become realigned with the fiends, while others, such as my father, wanted to keep a low profile until the day we were ready to take over the world on our own. Thus we split into two factions."

It was clear that she didn't want me to know about the trouble between her people, but now that I had seen it firsthand, she had no choice but to show me her cards. "So you and your father belong to a rebel faction, just like the People's Liberation Force?" I asked.

She laughed. "I guess you could call us something like that."

We continued along the ocean's rocky floor with a more cautious spring in our step, not wanting to be spotted by any hostile Shellians. "We almost there?"

"Almost," Fiona whispered as we came to a stop behind the cover of a large boulder.

She peered around the edge out into the open field of seaweed. A few fish lazily swam by, unaware of our presence until Fiona motioned to indicate that the coast was clear. We jogged out into the open toward the shore, the canopy of water above us getting closer and closer to our heads until finally we were there.

Fiona and I emerged from the ocean's grasp and waded our way to the beach where Grant and Lara waited to greet us. "I know there is nothing I could do to ever repay you for what you've done to save my life, but if you ever need anything, I will always be in your debt," I promised her.

"I'm sure one of these days I will take you up on that offer," she replied with a smirk.

"Hey, Babe!" came the cry as Lara waded her way out to us to give me a hug.

"Hey, it's so good to see you!" I replied with a kiss on her cheek.

She blushed, glancing over to Fiona. Respect filled Lara's eyes, completely opposite of when she had first met Fiona. "Thank you for everything you've done for us. If there is anything I can ever do for you, just say the word, and I'll be there," Lara told her.

"Will do," Fiona replied, extending her hand out to Lara, who gave it a firm shake.

I watched in disbelief. Never would I have thought I'd live to see the day that a Shellian and a fiend would shake each other's hands with respect for each other. "What's up, playa?" Grant greeted me as I came to the shore, escaping the icy grasp of the Atlantic Ocean for the first time in months.

Grant was my best friend in the people's liberation force, tall, athletic build with dark skin and a humour that could put a smile on anyone's face. When the fiends first invaded we met under the tutelage of Captain Murphy becoming inseparable. He was the only one I had left who had been there from the start.

"Not a whole lot," I called, glancing back at Lara and Fiona as they hugged each other in the surf.

"Isn't that a sight, eh?" Grant grunted.

I muttered my agreement, taking a seat beside him. "So what's new?"

"Too much to go over here," he replied with a laugh.

"Like what?"

"Well, for starters, there's a war going on between the fiends and the humans," he told me.

I laughed, giving him a playful punch to the shoulder. "Ain't been gone that long buddy."

"Bye, guys," Fiona called to us with a wave.

We returned it. Fiona and Lara shared their final good-byes. Then Fiona disappeared back into the surf. "Where to now?" I grunted once Lara had returned to us.

"Camp," she responded.

"Huh?" I asked her, confused.

A sly smile spread across her face. "You will see," she said, motioning for me to follow her.

Grant handed me a rifle. Then we began the long journey up the steep mountainside into the concealment of the forest above. It wasn't as long of a hike as I had thought, but the terrain was unforgiving. Less than an hour later, we were tucked away in the safety of the rebels' camp.

Lara led Grant and me across the camp to a shelter in the middle. "This is nice. You two built all this?" I asked.

Lara nodded. "It's not much, but it will do for now."

I couldn't help noticing that the small camp was entirely abandoned. "Is it just the three of us?"

Lara nodded.

"Where is Carana?" I asked, confused.

"Away," she responded.

"Huh?" I asked, Carana had been traveling with them after the ambush in Brawklin City which confused me as to why she was being so secretive.

"We have a lot to catch up on," Grant explained.

Lara nodded her agreement. "This way." She gestured toward a small hut in the center of the camp. "Welcome to the headquarters."

I had to duck to get into the small hut. The hut was about six feet high, and pine branches were serving as a roof. Inside was nothing but a few large rocks to serve as chairs and a small crate in the corner. I glanced at the charcoals in the middle of the hut, seeing that they were using this place to cook their food.

"Not exactly a lunar lake setup, huh?" Grant joked, referring back to our old camp of the People's Liberation Force.

I laughed.

"I know, it needs a lot of work," Lara commented defensively.

"It's a good start though," I reassured them.

Grant and Lara both nodded their agreement.

"So where's Carana?" I re asked.

They both shared a look with each other before Grant spoke up. "When you were hurt, we did some reconnaissance and found out that Rashellia was taken to a laboratory in South Lassetia. Carana, being a fiend with no known ties to us, was the best candidate to send as a spy."

"She's in there with Rashellia?" I asked, unable to contain the excitement in my voice.

"We don't know. We haven't heard from her," Lara said.

"What do you know, then?" I asked.

Lara gave me a gentle smile. She must have been able to tell I was getting frustrated. "We know she was accepted into the program as a trainee. We haven't heard from her since though."

I let out a sigh. At least there was a little bit of good news. "So what now?" I asked.

"We build the PLF in this area," Grant said.

I laughed. "You're not serious, are you?"

"Dead serious," he replied. "You and I have been through it; we know the ropes and have the skills to lead the men into battle. We will take the fight to the fiends and eventually be strong enough to rescue your daughter."

"Yeah, that sounds great and all. But what about Lara?" I began. "We are not going to have many supporters to fight the fiends when we have one living in our own camp."

"Deserters of the fiends could be integrated into the camp and rehabilitated to fight for us," she suggested.

"What about humans? They would be our main recruits."

Lara shrugged. "We won't tell them at first. I can pass as a darn good human," she replied with a grin.

I didn't find the joke amusing though. "I don't know. This seems like a dream more than anything," I muttered.

"Do you have a better idea?" Grant snapped.

I went silent.

"I'm sorry," he said

"It's fine. I am too. I shouldn't have been so negative," I replied.

"Are you ladies done yet?" Lara asked, trying to lighten the mood.

The three of us laughed. "So where do we begin?" I asked.

"Recruitment?" Grant suggested.

"It would probably be more enticing for them to join if we had a decent camp," Lara chimed in.

I couldn't help rolling my eyes. Not even thirty seconds after we had decided to go through with this plan, everyone was already butting heads. "Perhaps Grant and I could go recce out potential recruitment spots while you stay back and work on the camp," I offered to Lara.

"Yeah, I guess that's fine," she muttered. She folded her arms across her chest, which clearly said otherwise.

"How much weaponry and ammo do we have?" I asked them.

They both laughed. "You're looking at it," Grant said.

I laughed to myself. "Guess we are going to have to win this war with three rifles and about ninety rounds."

Lara shot me a smile. She uncovered a few pine furs lying on the floor, revealing my Timberwolf, which had been hidden underneath. "You didn't think I'd lose one of your most prized possessions, did you?"

I shot her a joyful look, picking up the weapon. I cocked it back to check the action of the sniper rifle. "Now we're talking," Grant said as I finished inspecting the weapon.

"That's enough resistance talk for now, boys. Grant and I are just happy to have you back," Lara whispered.

"Thanks, Babe."

"You're welcome," Grant replied playfully.

We all laughed. Lara reached behind her, opened up the crate, and pulled out three cans of kippers. "Food fit for a king," Grant muttered.

I couldn't help but smirk as I stared down at the small meal. We ate in silence, occasionally passing around the only canteen of water we had. Dusk began to set in around us as we finished off our meal.

Lara got up, retrieved some kindling from the small collection, and tossed it in the fire pit. With a snap of her fingers, a flame shot from her hand, igniting the kindling. "She has her uses, huh?" Grant asked.

I laughed.

"Shut your mouth," she said to him playfully.

She pulled her rock over to me and started to cuddle

affectionately. Grant let out a yawn. "Well, I'm beat. Going to call it a night, kids. I'll see you bright and early tomorrow," he said and gave Lara and me some time alone.

I shot him a thankful nod. He stuck a stick into the fire to use as his torch and then made his escape from the hut, calling out a final good night. "He's such a great guy," Lara said, returning her attention to me.

"You're such a great girl," I replied and placed a kiss on her cheek.

She giggled. "I love you, Lance."

"I love you more, Lara."

We cuddled for a little, accompanied only by the flickering flames of the small fire that made our shadows dance around the walls of the hut. Without a word she began to get undressed. There was nothing that needed to be said though. We both wanted it.

"I missed you so much," I whispered, sliding my hand across her bare skin until it came to a rest on her bum. She giggled and gave me a kiss.

I returned it, and we began to make out. "You're so amazing," she whispered.

Carrying her over to where a blanket was lying on the ground on top of a cluster of pine tree branches, I set her down and got on top as she slipped my shirt off. I unbuckled my pants, glancing over at the fire. She smiled. With a flick of her wrist the fire was extinguished, and the fire between Lara and I was reignited.

CHAPTER 4

I awoke the next morning to the soft chirping of birds outside. The pine-tree branches did not make for a comfortable sleep, but the blanket Lara and Grant had scavenged made a world of difference. I got up in silence and made my best attempt to not wake Lara up as I dressed, slung the assault rifle over my shoulder, and sneaked out.

It looked like it was going to be a beautiful day. The soft rays of sunlight beaming down through the tree branches seemed to dance off the morning mist below. Having some time to myself, I took a better look around camp.

There were three lean-to shelters, with the HQ hut in the middle. There was also a trail which led to the cliff that overlooked the ocean. I decided to follow it. Coming to a rest at the edge of the cliff, I took a seat and leaned back to soak in the picture of the vast blue ocean in front of me.

"How did you sleep, Lance?"

I glanced behind to see who the source of the voice was and spotted Grant coming down the path toward me. "It certainly isn't the Hilton Hotel," I told him.

He laughed, taking a seat by my side. "You all right?"

All I could offer was a shrug. "I can't get Rashellia off my mind, man."

He remained silent; I guess he didn't know what to say. Finally he answered, "It's not much, but at least she's safe. The firstborn half blood would be way too important for the fiends to kill."

I grunted my agreement. "But for how long?"

"We will get her back before that time comes," he replied.

I smiled, holding my hand out to him in a fist. He gave it a bump. "Thanks, man," I grunted.

He gave me a nod. "You know I've got your back."

Letting out a sigh, I returned my gaze to the ocean and watched the sun rise in the distance. "We're going to need a better path down there," I muttered to myself, staring at the beach.

"Huh?" Grant asked.

"It's going to be one of our primary sources of food," I explained.

"Aww," he replied.

"How far is it to the nearest lake?" I asked.

A smile spread across his face, probably as he realized that I was fully on board with building another resistance. "About a half-hour hike." He paused. "It's all downhill though."

"And all uphill on the way back," I added.

We both laughed. "It's good to have you back, Lance."

"It's good to be back," I replied.

We were both startled by the rustling of a bush behind us. Fearing it was a bear, I reached for my weapon. But it was only Lara, who emerged from the cover of the forest's vegetation.

"Oh, I see how it is," was her opening remark. "Don't invite the chick out anywhere, huh?"

The three of us laughed. She took a seat beside me, giving a morning kiss. "Did you have a good night?" she asked with a wink.

I smirked, returning the wink. "It might have been the best night ever."

"Oh, come on, guys. I'm right here!" Grant protested.

Lara and I shared a secret smile, and I gave her a light peck on the cheek before changing the subject for Grant's sake. "So what's for breakfast?" I asked.

"Crab apples," Lara replied.

"Huh? Don't they make you sick?" I asked.

Grant shrugged. "You can eat one or two a day, just not a whole bunch."

I gave him an unsure look, but after thinking about it, I came to the conclusion that being sick would beat starving. So the three of us got up, and Lara lead the way to the crab apple tree. It turned out to be right in front of our camp.

"Here you go, champ," Grant said, tossing one of the apples to me.

I stared at the dull green fruit, rotating it around in my hand and inspecting it for cleanliness. "Oh, come on, Babe. Just get it into you," Lara coaxed, a grin from ear to ear forming at my reluctance.

With the pure pressure mounting, I let out a sigh and took a bite. It wasn't as bad as I had thought. The sweet-sour taste seemed to make my dormant taste buds spring back to life as I took another bite.

"Mmm … It's all right, I guess," I admitted, staring at the apple.

"Attagirl," Grant replied.

"Always got to be the class clown, hey, Grant?" I asked.

He shrugged. "Comes natural, bro."

We all cracked up, and then we finished our apples and got down to business. "Well, I guess I'll work on building the structure for the medical hut ... You boys be safe out there," Lara said, getting up and wiping the dirt off her pants.

"Thanks, Babe," I replied and gave her a good-bye kiss.

Grant and I picked up our assault rifles and loaded a magazine each before putting the weapons on safe. I glanced at him, and he gave me a nod. "Ladies first," he said.

I laughed, taking the lead. As we navigated our way through the forest to the nearest village, which was about ten to thirteen kilometers away from our camp, Grant marked our track by cutting into the bases of tree trunks with his hunting knife—a safety precaution in case we lost our way back. As noon approached, the brutal summer heat swiftly followed.

"Damn mosquitoes," Grant grunted, swatting at his neck as we stopped for a break about a kilometer from the village.

"Almost there," I replied. I took a drink from our canteen and then held it out to him.

"Thanks," he muttered, took a drink, and tucked it away in his pocket. "So how's it feel being back, doing what we do best?"

"Just like riding a bike," I said, a grin spreading across my face.

He grunted in agreement. "Don't think you ever lose it."

I nodded and took a quick glance at the map. "Ready?"

"Always," he replied.

It didn't take much longer for us to arrive at the outskirts of the village. Grant and I crested the top of a small berm, where we took cover behind a few shrubs and peered through at the village below. At first glance, the village appeared to be abandoned. "No one's home," Grant said.

I brought my finger to my lips, pointing down to the village. His eyes followed my finger and spotted what I had just discovered: the remains of a small campfire. All that was left of it was the smoldering ashes, indicating that whoever had made it had left in a hurry.

"Do you hear that?" Grant whispered.

I strained my head toward the village. I could hear the very distant sound of a crying child inside one of the houses. "Could be a trap," I warned.

"We've got to check it out though," Grant debated.

I wanted to argue that it wasn't worth the risk, but I could see the passion in Grant's eyes. He had clearly already made his decision. I knew him all too well; if I didn't go with him, he would go by himself, no matter what.

"Okay, let's do it. Be careful," I whispered.

We left our cover and trotted down to the village, slowing to a walking pace with our weapons at the low ready as we reached the outskirts of town. It was then that we realized the village was nothing more than a grave. "The fiends got them all," I whispered.

Grant nodded as we walked by a dead family that had been gruesomely devoured in the middle of the street. "Not all of them," he corrected, staring at the house the cries were coming from.

"I'll go in," I said, reaching for the door handle. "You cover out here."

My palms were sweating profusely as I gripped the door handle. I gave it a turn and was rewarded by the dull creak of the hinges swinging open. The child's cries went silent.

I gave Grant a pat on the back and then entered, gun at the ready.

"Hello?" I called out almost in a whisper.

No one answered. The room's only light came from the sun's rays stealing through the lone shattered window of the house. "Hello?" I re called out.

Silence.

I slowly made my way across the living room and found the source of the crying in the hallway to the kitchen. "Hi buddy," I whispered, reaching my hand out to a child of about six or seven years old.

He recoiled from me and quivered uncontrollably in fear as he gripped his dead mother's body lying next to him. Her throat had been slit. I knew the fiends all too well. These monsters hadn't left the child alive as an act of mercy; they wanted him to watch his mother die so he would fear the fiends for the rest of his life.

Offering my hand to the child again, I whispered, "I'm not here to hurt you."

He gulped and glanced at his mother before coming to me. As he approached, the light shone across his face, revealing the long slash of a fiend's claw from his ear down to his chin. It would be a constant reminder for him of this day.

"Grant, I need your help!" I called out. He was carrying what little medical supplies we had.

Grant came barreling through the door like a bull, probably thinking I was in trouble. He stopped abruptly at my side, realizing it wasn't what he had thought.

"Hey, don't worry, buddy. We'll fix you up," he said, his voice softening as he knelt down to the kid's level and pulled out a rag.

I watched in silence as he poured some water on the cloth and wiped away the blood from the child's cut as well as he could. "All better?"

The kid gave Grant a halfhearted smile. "Attaboy," Grant said and patted him on the shoulder.

I jerked my head toward the kid's mother, and Grant's stare shifted, a look of disgust spreading across his face to the sight of what they had done to her and her son. "Damn monsters."

I nodded my agreement. "What's your name?" I asked the child.

"Joshua," he whispered.

"I'm Lance, and this is Grant."

He glanced from me to Grant, fear still written in his eyes. It was clear that it was going to take a lot of rehab to help him recover. All I could hope was that Lara's motherly touch would be enough.

"Were there any hunters in your village before all of this, Joshua?"

The boy nodded. "Uncle Ben," he whispered, pointing to the house behind the one we were in.

I signalled for Grant to go retrieve the rifle; Grant obediently got up and left the child and me in silence. I felt like a grave robber, stealing a dead man's gun, but we would need it more than he did now.

"Are you hungry?" I asked Joshua.

He nodded, so I helped him up, put my hand on his back, and guided him to the kitchen. They didn't have much food that wouldn't go bad in a few days. I made Joshua a ham sandwich to preoccupy him. Then I pulled a bag out of my pocket and stuffed it with canned fruit, tuna, kippers, and the like.

"How is it?" I asked him as I scurried around the kitchen, trying to find other supplies, though I only discovered scissors and a roll of string.

"Good." He was staring down the hall at his mother.

"My mother died when I was very young too, Joshua."

"Did the fiends kill her?"

I shook my head. "She died of a disease called cancer before the war. I thought my life was over, but you know what I realized?"

"What?"

"She would want me to be happy."

Without warning, his eyes began to tear up. "But I miss her so much!" he sniffled.

"I know; I know you do." All I could offer was a pat on his back, not having much skill with children. He pulled me close though, burying his face in my chest, and then began to bawl.

"Shh, shh. It's going to be okay," I said.

I glanced up at the sounds of footsteps. Grant appeared, the hunting rifle shouldered together with his assault rifle now. He held up a shovel and pickax he had found, a triumphant smile plastering his face. It faded, however, as he stared at the sobbing child in my arms. "We have to go," he mouthed to me.

I nodded, waving him away. Staring down at the child, I couldn't help but think about Rashellia. "You're going to have to be a big boy now, Joshua," I told him.

He gave me a nod, hiccupping as he wiped away a tear. "I need you to go outside with Grant, okay? I'll be right out."

He did so obediently, taking one last look at his mother as he stepped over her lifeless body. I shouldered my assault rifle, picked up the bag of food, and followed his trail to the door. I paused to kneel down at his mother's side.

She had a knife in her hand, probably to protect Joshua. She hadn't gone down without a fight; that was for sure. I closed her eyes. "I'll take care of him," was all I could think to say. Without another word I got up and met Grant and Joshua outside.

The hike back took twice as long. My throat was parched, since I'd forgone my share of water in order to accommodate Joshua.

"Hey there, strangers. Welcome back!" Lara called as Grant and I appeared back in camp. Her eyes widened as Joshua appeared from behind us. "Well, hello there," she added to him, taking a knee.

I nudged him toward her. "It's okay. She won't hurt you."

As he walked forward, Lara opened her arms to him. *"He's hurt,"* she whispered into my head through our telepathic connection. *"I could heal it,"* she added.

"Would it prevent the scarring?"

"No."

I closed my eyes, feeling terrible that this child would be scarred by the fiends for the rest of his life. *"Don't do it, then. His family was just killed by fiends. You may frighten him,"* I replied in my head.

She smiled at the child, patting his long dirty-blond hair away from his eyes.

"What's your name?" he asked Lara.

"Lara." She paused. "What's yours?"

"Joshua," he replied.

She beamed down at him. "How old are you, Joshua?"

"Seven," he told her, counting it out on his fingers and then holding them out to her.

I glanced at Grant. He had his arms folded across his chest and a dull smile on his face.

"Are you hungry?" Lara asked him.

He shook his head. "Lance made me lunch at my mommy's house," he told her.

She smiled at me. I returned it. I could tell she had already fallen in love with the boy. Lara was a great mother; it came naturally to her.

"Well, let's go see if we can find you somewhere to sleep," she said, leading Joshua to the HQ hut.

"She's great, hey?" I asked.

Grant nodded. "I almost forget sometimes that she's a fiend."

"Get on her bad side, and you will remember real quick," I told him.

He laughed. The two of us walked around the camp. Lara had constructed another lean-to and had begun to form the structure of our medical hut. "Well, this lean-to would probably make a good shelter for supplies," I remarked.

We placed the goods in there and then walked back to the HQ hut. Lara swiftly brought her finger to her mouth as we entered. I glanced down at Joshua, who was fast asleep in her arms.

"Poor little guy's beat," Grant whispered.

She nodded, with a caring twinkle in her eyes, and then returned her attention to Joshua, stroking his hair affectionately.

"He's not the only one," I added, stifling a yawn.

Grant grunted his agreement to my statement, taking a seat on a rock. He set his assault rifle and the hunting rifle we had acquired up against the wall of the hut. I placed mine beside the other two weapons and sat down between him and Lara.

"I thought you were going to come back with fighters," she whispered to Grant and me.

I rolled my eyes, spotting the playful smile on her face.

"So did I," Grant replied.

"It's not like we could just leave him there to die," I argued.

"This place isn't much safer," Lara replied.

"We will be fine," I said, dismissing her statement.

Grant went silent, I guess not wanting any more of this conversation.

"Every time you save a life you take responsibility for it, Lance," Lara pursued. "We can't accommodate the wounded, elderly, and children. We can barely take care of ourselves."

"We will go back to the village tomorrow and gather more supplies," I told her.

She fell silent.

"We can do this," I promised her. "It's not just about fighting the war. It's about protecting the innocent."

She paused, taking another look at Joshua. I knew she wanted fighters. I did too. We weren't going to be able to rescue Rashellia with a snap of our fingers. It would take time, lots of time. I just hoped she would realize that.

"You're right," she whispered.

"Wow." Grant laughed. "It's not every day a woman says that."

The three of us laughed, waking Joshua up.

"I'm thirsty," he whispered to Lara.

I handed the canteen to her, which he emptied.

"Do we even have any fresh water?" I asked Grant.

He nodded. "Not a lot though. It hasn't rained in forever."

He exited the hut momentarily and returned with a bowl of water and four tins of kippers. "The water's going to need to be boiled to kill any bacteria," Lara reminded us.

I got up, collected the last of the kindling from the corner of the hut, and threw it into the fire pit. Lara was about to lean forward to start the fire, but I shooed her away, nodding toward Joshua. She backed off, realizing she had almost blown her cover, and gave me a thankful nod.

"You got a lighter, Grant?" I asked.

He shook his head. I reached into my pocket, pulling out a half-full box of matches I had found in Joshua's house. I struck the first one, which snapped in half.

They were in pretty bad shape, I realized, breaking three more. "Come on," I whispered to myself, pulling out another match as the box's contents continued to dwindle.

The sound of this match striking the box was rewarded with a sizzle as a flame lit it up. I threw it on the fire and blew gently as the kindling began to smolder. A flame flickered up from the wood. "Good job, Babe," Lara said, handing me a log.

I put it on the fire and then returned to my seat.

"Need a hand with that?" Lara asked Joshua, who was struggling to open his tin of kippers.

He nodded, and she opened it for him. "Thank you," he muttered, digging into the fish.

The three of us followed his lead, eating in silence. Afterward, Grant and I took turns holding a bowl of water by the edge of its handles over the fire, which took about fifteen minutes to boil. "'Bout time," Grant grunted, taking the bowl off the fire to cool.

"I'll catch you guys tomorrow, then," Grant said, getting up to leave.

"No, wait. The air is pretty moist out there. It may rain. Why don't you spend the night in here with us," Lara suggested.

He looked like he was about to decline the offer when, as if on cue, the dull pattering of rain could be heard outside. We laughed. "Well, I guess if you're going to twist a man's arm," he joked, taking off his shirt to serve as a pillow and searching for a flat piece of ground to lie on.

Lara brought Joshua to the pile of pine branches, laid the blanket on top, and then tucked him in. She turned to leave, but Joshua grabbed hold of her hand, pulling her back. She leaned down, and he whispered something into her ear.

"I won't," she promised, with a reassuring smile. She placed a kiss on the child's forehead, took off her shirt, and tucked it under his head as a pillow. "Sweet dreams, Joshua."

I placed my jacket on the hard ground, took off my shirt to use as a blanket for the two of us, and lay down. Lara joined me soon after, wrapping her arms around me to cuddle. After I gratefully accepted her into my arms, we were rewarded with the warmth of each other's body heat. I gave her a confused glance as I felt her body trembling. Her face was pale as a ghost, but she shooed my concern away with a gentle kiss.

"What's wrong, Babe?"

"Nothing," she whispered.

Her body stopped shaking. As her muscles tensed up, however, I could tell that she was forcing it to.

"Please don't tell me you're starting your tricnoses," I whispered back.

She smiled. "I just need blood. That's all."

"How long has it been?"

"Two weeks."

My eyes widened. "Two weeks!"

That was way too long for a fiend to go without blood. She was unstable. Now she could transform at any time. "Here," I closed my eyes, offering my wrist under the blanket.

"Lance!"

"Just do it, Lara."

"No, I can't. I'll go hunting by myself tomorrow," she whispered.

"That won't tide you over for long. You've said it yourself—human blood is the purest," I said, forcing her to draw my blood.

She closed her eyes. I cringed in pain while the razor-sharp fangs sank into my wrist. Blood was dripping down her lips as my wrist went numb. She finished quickly and ran her hand along my wrist, which healed the damage within seconds.

"Thank you," she whispered.

I could see the apologetic look in her eyes. "It's fine, Babe. Don't worry."

She gave me a halfhearted smile. I could already see the color returning to her face, restoring her beautiful complexion. I smiled, hugging her close to me. We settled back into our sleeping arrangement as the grogginess of sleep set in.

"What did Joshua whisper to you?" I asked.

"Huh?"

"When you were tucking him in."

"Oh ..." She hesitated. I stared at her, confused. She gave me an embarrassed shrug. "He said, 'Please don't let the fiends take me away.'"

CHAPTER 5

It had rained long and hard the night before. As Grant and I got ready for our excursion back to the village, I glanced over at the two now-full water buckets sitting by the structure of the medical hut. I couldn't help but smile, satisfied that things were going our way for once.

I felt a tug on my pant leg and glanced down at Joshua. "Where are you going?" he asked.

"Just for a walk with Grant. We will be back this afternoon," I replied, shouldering the assault rifle.

"Joshua?" Lara called to him. His attention shifted to her as she emerged from the HQ hut. "You want to help me make some beds so Lance and Grant have somewhere to sleep tonight?" she asked.

Joshua nodded and raced to the hut. She gave him a playful pat on the back, nodding him into the hut. She came over to me as he disappeared behind the hut's door. "He's not too much of a burden on you, is he?" I asked.

"Not at all!" she objected with an offended tone in her voice.

"You're so wonderful around him ... I can see the life returning back already."

She smiled. "You be careful out there."

I nodded. She got up on her tippy toes and gave me a kiss.

"Love you, Babe," I whispered.

"Love you too." she giggled.

"See you boys tonight," she called with a wink to me. Then she turned and disappeared into the hut with Joshua.

Knowing the way to Joshua's village made the journey so much easier that it almost cut in half the time it took to get there.

"Jesus," Grant grunted.

I turned to see him lying on the ground, tangled in some of the many branches that littered the Harush Forest. Chuckling to myself, I offered him a hand, asking, "Are you all right?"

He nodded, brushing the pine needles off his clothes, and picked up his weapon. "I'll tell you one thing: If we're recruiting fiends, then they're going to be carrying my ass everywhere we go. I'm getting too old for this walk-thirty-kilometers-a-day business," he muttered.

"You're twenty-three," I replied.

"Twenty-three going on fifty," came the disgruntled response.

We both laughed and stopped for a water break and a quick check of the map. It took us less than thirteen more minutes to reach the village. There was an unfamiliar feeling in the air as we entered. Grant put his hand across my chest, stopping me from going any further. He pointed to the abandoned deck of a cabin in front of us. I shot him a confused look.

"Last time I checked, dead people don't get up and walk away," he whispered.

I glanced back at the deck, my memory returning of the dead bodies strewn across this village. Something was definitely wrong.

"Let's get out of here," I whispered back.

It was too late though. A warning shot rang out behind us. We turned around and were greeted by the sight of three middle-aged men, two of which had us at gunpoint.

"All right, ladies. Hands up," the oldest of the three called out.

I glanced at Grant before returning my gaze to the approaching men. "Just do it," I grunted.

Grant and I obediently threw our weapons to the ground and raised our hands. These weren't professional soldiers but perhaps hunters or bandits. Each man's face was covered by a greasy, undaunted beard. I could make out their thick country accent as they argued about something among themselves.

"What business you boys got here?" one of them asked. He spat a lugy onto the ground, staring at us.

"Just passing through," I muttered.

"There isn't nothing to see here, boy. Just carnage and death. Dem fiends came through and killed everyone," he told us.

I relaxed a bit, realizing that these men posed no threat to us. "We know. Not everyone was killed. There was a child that survived."

He stared at us a moment, I guess deciding whether we were friend or foe. At a nod of his head, his two men lowered their weapons.

"What ya got there?" he asked, nodding at our weapons on the ground.

"Oh, these are just M4s. An old assault rifle but still

great for killing fiends," I replied as Grant and I picked them up.

"Can I take a gander?" he asked.

Against my better judgment, I unloaded the weapon and handed it to him. The three of them huddled around it like a group of kids trying out a new toy for the first time.

"Dem boys be fiend killers."

I glanced at Grant. A look of indifference was written on his face. Feeling the same lack of interest in being around these hillbillies, I politely asked for my weapon back.

"Oh yes, sir," he said, handing it back. "Jack, Luey, and Steve at your service," he said with a smile on his face. "We be fiend killers too."

It took everything I had to hold back laughter.

"You three are resistance fighters?" I asked.

"Resistance fighters? What them boys be talking about?" one of them asked. The others shrugged.

I saw Grant roll his eyes. "How many fiends have you guys killed?" he asked in amusement.

"Three or four," Steve replied in his thick accent. "My brothers and I be passing through these lands when we seen these poor folk dead as a winter crop. Couldn't leave them to rot. We've been working all day."

He motioned for us to follow them and led us to the back of the village where they had constructed a cemetery. "Just dat one lady left, and they all be buried."

I glanced at the body lying by a half-dug hole. It was Joshua's mother.

"My friend and I will take care of this last one," I said.

"Huh?" Grant asked.

I gave him a sharp prod in the ribs, shutting him up.

"Dank you, kind sirs. We will be off, then," Steve told us.

I nodded, my respect for the three men having increased significantly. "I wish you the best on your journey," I told them, offering my hand.

Steve nodded, giving it a firm shake. "Same to you, kind sir."

The trio then grabbed their gear and headed up the mountain opposite of where Grant and I had come from.

"Why are we grave diggers now?" Grant asked.

"This is Joshua's mother," I explained.

He went silent, taking another look at the woman. I saw the realization cross his eyes.

"Guess I should grab a shovel, eh?"

I nodded; he wandered off in search of one. I took off my jacket, grasped the shovel stuck in the hole, and began to dig out the grave at a brisk pace, not wanting to spend much time there. The more time Grant and I spent doing this, the less time for us to collect supplies.

Grant appeared a short time later with a shovel. "Found an ax for the camp too!" he called over, holding it up in his other hand.

I flashed him a quick smile, nodding toward the grave for his help. We worked in silence, finishing in less than twenty minutes. "Should we say a few words?" I asked after placing her body in the grave.

Grant shrugged. "What can we say? We don't know her."

To a normal person his words would sound harsh, but after being in the resistance for so long, we had grown accustomed to death.

"Yeah, you're probably right," I muttered.

We filled in the grave, shouldered our rifles, and grabbed the extra supplies to take back to camp. I followed Grant over to the barn where he had discovered the ax and shovel.

There was a bucket of nails, some mallets, and a measuring tape—all stuff that could be useful for making shelters.

It only took us about five minutes to gather the supplies, but that was all that was needed for the weather outside to take a turn for the worse.

"Shit," I muttered, staring up at the sky as dark clouds rolled in.

"Too bad none of these folk believed in rain jackets," Grant grunted to himself, following my stare.

The journey back was nothing short of miserable. The rain intensified to the point where the ground around us was transformed into a river. Periodically, thunder would boom out overhead, followed by a couple of flashes of lightning lighting up the sky. All I could think about was Joshua and Lara, hoping the shelter would weather the storm.

"Hold up a second," Grant called, raising his hand.

He took a seat and took off his boot. It was like a bucket of water being poured out. I laughed, wiping the water away from my own eyes with my sopping wet hunting attire before we set off again toward camp, fearing the worst.

Arriving back in camp a short time later and expecting to see the place in ruins, we couldn't have been any more wrong. Grant and I stared at Joshua and Lara in disbelief as we watched the two of them having the time of their lives in the rain. "You little bugger!" Lara yelled, chasing after him. He stomped in the puddle in front of her, sending water flying. She giggled, chasing him around a hut. She finally caught him and dunked him into the same puddle. Then they both stopped, realizing we had returned.

Lara dug around in the mud and formed a ball with her hand. The two of them then stared at us innocently.

"Hey!" I warned her, pointing a stern finger at them. "Put the mud down."

Joshua whispered something into her ear. She nodded in agreement. The mud ball hit me square in the chest, giving them all the time they needed. "Aww!" they cried, charging toward us. I barely had enough time to brace myself before Lara and Joshua collided with me.

"Get his leg," she yelled, holding my arms away.

The tug on my leg made me fall to the ground. Lara got on top of me and sprayed mud all over. A smile from ear to ear formed on her face.

Grant came to my aid, but it was too little too late. "Get off him, you little monster!" he called, playfully picking up Joshua.

"Roarrr!" Joshua cried, hugging him close and trying to take him to the ground.

Grant allowed him to, and the pair play-fought as Lara's and my fight turned into a make-out session. "Love you," I whispered, hugging her close. She purred and gave me another kiss.

"Eww!" I heard and glanced at Grant and Joshua. A disgusted look was on the child's face. We all laughed.

"Get a room!" Grant called over to us.

"Lance has girl cooties," Joshua added.

"What!" Lara called back over to the child.

Grant wrapped his arms around Joshua before the poor kid had time to put up a struggle. "Agh!" he cried, holding his hands out.

It was too late though. Grant and I dragged him to the ground and proceeded to tickle him as Lara smothered his forehead with kisses. "Now who has girl cooties?"

Joshua smiled, giving Lara a big hug. "I love you, Lara."

Grant and I both got up, looking down at them. Lara hugged him close. I could see the motherly side of her taking over as she gave him another kiss on the forehead. "I love you too, Joshua."

Grant and I helped them up and found shelter in the hut where I built a small fire. Lara was super affectionate. She kept rubbing my leg and giving me kisses, not taking her eyes off me once.

"Want to go for a walk?" she asked.

I nodded; the two of us excused ourselves. Once we were outside, she held my hand, our fingers intertwining with one another's as we walked to the camp's edge. We stared at each other in silence as the rain pounded against our skin. The cool moistness replaced the grainy feeling of dirt.

She closed her eyes for a moment, resting her head against my chest. I rubbed her back, feeling the tense muscles relax. She took off her clothes and held out her hand.

I gave her a confused smile, holding mine out as well. She giggled and led me into the forest. I ran my hand along her body, feeling every curve of it. She slapped it away with a playful smirk. "Bad boy."

Her muscles started to contract and tighten. Her bones were cracking. "What are you doing?" I asked.

"Don't be scared," she replied.

She took a step back and dropped to all fours. She let out a cry of anguish as her backbone shot out. Skin was ripped away and replaced with the dark-scaled fiend skin, patches of fur spreading all over her body. Within moments, the transformation was complete.

I stared at her elegant fiend form. It had been a long time since I had seen her like this. She bowed her gigantic head and lay down on the ground as I ran my hand along her long, furry body.

"Been a while, huh?" she asked, her voice echoing through my head.

Giving her a nod, I got on top instantly. I was greeted by the warmth of her body as I wrapped my arms around her massive neck, feeling the sheer power course through her body as she got to her feet. She launched us into the air. It was rough at first, probably from being so long since our last flight together, but we soon found a thermal. She extended her massive wings, and we began to glide southeast. As time continued to pass by, I realized this trip was more than just a fun flight.

"Where are we going, Lara?"

"South Lassetia."

Becoming more alert to my surroundings, I hunkered close to her body. I ignored the wind smashing against my face as I picked out prominent landmarks, knowing I would have to make this trip more than once. It was a half-hour flight away, so about a two-day walk. As we drew nearer, Lara descended to just above the canopy of the forest, fearing enemy patrols.

Shortly afterward, we landed in the tall, untouched grass of a meadow nearby. Staying in her fiend form, she carried me to the outskirts of the laboratory, where we found cover in the surrounding vegetation.

"This place looks like Fort Knox," I said.

The entire place was surrounded by a solid concrete wall. The only way in or out was over a medieval-looking bridge and then through a four- or five-inch-thick steel gate surrounded by a mote. There was an insane amount of security. I watched three fiends in their nonhuman form

44

THE UNEXPECTED WAR

patrol by. Guards in their human form manned guard towers, and the entire perimeter was laced with security cameras.

"It's not going to be any picnic getting in there," she told me.

I nodded. *"Not going to be any picnic getting out either,"* was all I could say.

We headed back to the meadow we had come from. I couldn't help being gripped by anger, knowing that my daughter was just behind those doors and that there was nothing I could do about it. After seeing the place, I now had doubts of whether we would even see her again. I glanced up at Lara's towering body. She had gone silent. I could only imagine that the feeling was mutual.

"I wanted you to see it for yourself," she finally said, halfway back to camp.

The rain had lightened to a dull patter, but it hadn't lifted my spirits at all. *"There's a lot of security, Lara."*

We went on in silence A few minutes passed before a lake began to appear ahead. She glided down to it, skimming the surface before landing at the edge. Her fur immediately began to shed, and the hard, scaly, black complexion of her skin faded to white.

It was beautiful to watch her transform. Within a blink of an eye, it was complete, leaving the naked figure of the girl I had fallen in love with. Our hands met as we walked up the wet beach. We came to a rest under a large oak tree.

We cuddled in silence for a while. I returned her kisses, but I'd never been good at hiding my emotions from her.

"Are you all right?" she whispered and gave me another kiss.

I returned it. "Just thinking."

"About?"

I shrugged. "Rashellia."

"I miss her," she whispered.

"We would need an entire army to take that place."

"Or the greatest sniper alive," she replied, running her hand along my cheek in affection.

I chuckled. "Good luck finding that guy."

She turned to face me and rested her chest against mine as she unbuttoned my shirt. "You've never had a problem finding my target."

The sex was great. I knew Lara all too well. It was her way of fixing things. Having sex with me would make everything magically all right, in her mind, but that wasn't the case.

The thoughts were still racing through my head of how we were going to rescue Rashellia, not to mention of the upcoming winter that we had to survive. I was forced to put these thoughts aside though, placing a fake smile on my face and following her into the lake to wash off.

"I love you so much," she whispered, sifting her hands through my hair. "I know you will find a way to get her out, Lance. You just need to believe in yourself as much as I believe in you."

"I will," I promised her. "One day we will see her again."

Her smile was almost as bright as the rising moon's reflection bouncing off the still water all around us. The short trip back to camp was in silence but not the same silence we had been plagued by before. Now refocused and reenergized, we knew what we had to do.

No one could stop us.

CHAPTER 6

"**I** got one! I got one!" came the excited cry of Joshua. I opened an eye and glanced down the beach to the young boy as he frantically began rolling in the fishing line tied around a solid stick. "Keep going, buddy! Bring him in," I called.

I stretched out my stiff joints, got up, wiped the sand off, and then strolled down to the beach. Putting a hand on Joshua's back, I said, "Looks like he's a big one."

Joshua nodded his agreement. My encouraging words seemed to speed him up reeling in the line, sweat pouring down his forehead.

"Keep it up, buddy," I called to him. I waded into the ocean and was greeted by the cool, refreshing feeling of the gentle waves lapping against my legs.

I spotted the pollock go streaking by, and I chased after it. With a dive, I caught the fishing line in my hands. I yanked the fish out of the water and held it up to Joshua. He began jumping around on the shoreline victoriously.

The fish continued to thrash around in my hands, but it was to no avail. I waded back to shore and handed the slippery fish over to Joshua, who stared down at it in joy. "That's at least a three pounder," I congratulated him.

He beamed at me and attached the hook to the end of the stick. The two of us made our way back up to the blanket we had set up above the shoreline.

"Can you help me fold this, Joshua?"

He nodded, handing me the finished product. "Grant and Lara are going to be so happy," he said.

I tied a rope around my waist and then his giving him a pat on his back, signaling that I was ready to go. Climbing the steep, rocky path up to the camp was always nothing short of a chore.

"Slow down, Joshua," I warned him.

He obediently waited for me. I glanced back down at the beach. One wrong step, and it would be game over. He was too young to understand that, so I had to constantly remind him of the danger.

Reaching the top a few minutes later, I untied the rope and coiled it around my shoulder. Then Joshua took off and sprinted toward the camp. I threw the blanket over my other shoulder and chased after him. He tried to lock himself into the HQ hut, but I was too quick.

"Uh-oh! The tickle monster's got you!" I yelled, wrestling him to the ground.

"Nooo!" he cried, laughing uncontrollably.

By the time I let him get to his feet, his face was turning red. We both took a seat on a log, and I offered him some water from the canteen. He accepted it and took a deep, long drink.

"When will Lara and Grant be back?" he asked.

All I could offer was a shrug. I had been chosen for babysitting duties while they went out scouting a village a little further east of the one where we had found Joshua. It had been two weeks since our excursion to South Lassetia, but it was still fresh in my mind as I anxiously sat around camp, praying that Grant and Lara would return with recruits.

I tossed the dead fish in a bowl of water to keep it fresh and retook my seat on the log to keep an eye on Joshua. He had found a stick to occupy himself with by playing soldier. With a sigh, I leaned back on the log, fighting sleep.

This was definitely not my highlight of the war, but at least it was a beautiful day. The only wind was a soft breeze that swayed the leaves back and forth. Birds flew by, singing their songs, the sound peacefully flowing to my ears.

The snapping of twigs brought my attention back. There was a full-grown buck standing about a hundred meters away on the outskirts of the camp, nibbling on a patch of grass. Instinctively, I reached for the hunting rifle by my side. A deer of that size could feed us for weeks. The realization soon kicked in that I couldn't kill it though.

"Lance, look. It's a big deer!" Joshua's excited cry rang out.

With a sigh, I released my hand from the weapon and brought a finger up to my mouth, motioning him over. The deer went stiff, and its head perked up, staring at us, as Joshua took a seat beside me on the log. "That's a big deer," he whispered.

I nodded. The deer returned to grazing on the grass, I guess not deeming us a threat—a mistake many deer had made before.

"He's called a buck."

"A buck?" Joshua asked.

I nodded. "That's what you call a male deer."

"What about a girl deer?"

"You would call that a doe. You can tell the difference by their horns. See those big ones?" I asked, pointing at the deer. "Female deer don't have those big horns."

"Cool."

I smiled, returning my attention to the deer. It hung around for a few more minutes and then sauntered off, disappearing back into the forest.

"Aww, come back, deer," Joshua said.

The look of disappointment across the small boy's face was priceless. I gave his back a pat. "Don't worry, buddy. You will see plenty more."

A short time later, the cracking sounds of twigs could be heard heading in our direction. I brought the rifle to my lap—just in case. Lara was the first to appear, followed by Grant and then two other men around our age.

"Lara!" Joshua cried out. He sprang off of the log and bounded over to her where they met with a hug. "Come look at the big fish me and Lance caught."

He grabbed her hand and took her to the bowl the dead fish was sitting in. "Oh boy, he's big!" Lara said.

Joshua smiled at her. I got up to greet our two visitors with a firm handshake.

"Smith and Ryan, this is Lance," Grant said, introducing us.

We shared a smile with each other. They looked like fit soldiers. Each was armed with a handgun and an assault rifle.

"Where are you guys from?" I asked.

"Ninth Mountain Infantry. We were doing a patrol a few days ago when we were ambushed," Smith began, glancing down in sorrow. "My brother and I were the only ones who survived."

"I'm sorry to hear that. It's good to have you guys on board though. We were hurting real bad for men," I told them.

They glanced around the camp. I could see the disinterest in Ryan's face, "Wipe that look off," Smith grunted, giving his brother a hard jab in the ribs.

He did so obediently. I smiled, pretending to ignore Ryan's rudeness and gesturing them past the HQ hut to the lean-tos we had built.

"You can stay here until you build your own hut," I explained to them. "There is no size limit for your shelter, but use common sense. If you build a castle out of wood or something that can easily be spotted by enemy air patrols, we are going to tell you to tear it down. The three of us are pretty easygoing, and there're not many camp rules. Just basic stuff like using the outhouse, no pissing in the woods, keeping up to par with your hygiene to prevent sickness, and stuff like that."

They nodded. I gave them a smile. "Any questions?"

Ryan cleared his throat, shifting around in place. "Um ... well, I hate to ask, but what's with the kid?"

"We found him in a village west of yours. The fiends had torn through, killing everything in their path. They killed his mother in front of his own eyes and then slashed his face so he would always have the reminder of that day. We couldn't leave him there to die. He's a good kid who deserves a shot at life," I explained.

They remained silent. There wasn't any argument that they could make, even if they disagreed with his presence in a rebel camp.

"So you guys hungry?" I asked as a way to break the silence.

"Yeah, we haven't eaten since the ambush," Smith answered.

"Well, then follow me; no one starves in this camp," I told them in an attempt to lighten the mood.

The three of us laughed, heading back to HQ. Grant was hunched over a rock, filleting the fish and flanked by Joshua, who was pacing back and forth.

"You hungry, dude?" Ryan asked.

Joshua nodded.

I rolled my eyes with a laugh. "Quit being a drama queen. You had lunch not even three hours ago."

He shrugged with smile, rubbing his stomach before his attention shifted back to the fish.

"I don't know where he puts it," I said, trying to make conversation.

Smith laughed. "My boy never stopped eating either."

"How old is he?"

"He's dead."

Grant glanced at me. I went silent, not pursing the conversation any further. "Sorry," I finally whispered.

He shook my apology away with his hand. "Don't worry about it. He was a good kid. I wouldn't want him to grow up through this," he told me with a shrug. "Have you ever had a kid?"

The smile I'd had on my face instantly vanished at the question. "She was taken away from me by the fiends." I felt it best not to mention that the reason she was taken was because she was a half blood.

"What was her name?"

"Rashellia. What about your boy's?"

"Donald," he replied.

I gave him a firm nod, which he returned. A mutual

respect for each another had definitely grown, making me glad to have taken the time to get to know him.

"Good to go?" I asked Grant.

He nodded, picking up the five fillets he had cut and throwing the excess skin and guts into the forest. The six of us huddled around the fire, watching the fillets cook as our shadows danced around the flickering fire.

As we cleaned our weapons, I couldn't help noticing that Ryan kept glancing at me. I sent him a confused look. He immediately looked away, but not even a moment later I caught him glancing at me again.

"What's up?" I asked.

"I know you," he muttered.

"Doubt it."

He laughed. "Not in person, but I've heard stories about you."

I glanced up from the rifle I was cleaning.

"You're that sniper—best in the war, they used to say. Rumor has it, though, you were captured about two years ago. So how are you here?" he asked.

I shook my head, looking back down at the weapon. "Think you got the wrong guy, partner."

He whispered something in his brother's ear. I could tell that he wasn't going to let it go. Ryan glanced from Lara to me and then to Grant.

"No ... don't lie to me. I know how the story goes. You were his right-hand man in the People's Liberation Force," he said, waving a finger at Grant. "You both survived the fiends' assault in the Harush Forest when India Company was destroyed. So how did you escape the prison? There's no way you could have survived the interrogations."

I stared at him, setting the hunting rifle on the ground

with a sigh. "Hey, Grant and Joshua, could you do me a favor and go collect some firewood?" I asked, dipping a stick into the fire and handing it over to Grant to use as a torch.

"But—" Joshua began to protest.

"Come on, buddy. It will be fun," Grant said, getting up and leading him outside.

My attention returned to Ryan. He knew he was right. I wanted so badly to wipe that arrogant smile off his face though. Leaning forward, I motioned for him to come closer and said quietly, "It's not hard to survive a prison when your interrogator falls in love with you."

His eyes widened as he shot up, glancing from me to Lara with the final piece of the puzzle falling into place. "Buu … what? You're a fiend?!" he exclaimed.

She smiled, her eyes boiling blood red, and razor-sharp teeth ripping from her mouth. The two of them started up in fear. But I held up my hand, she returned to normal, and we both shared a laugh at them.

"I'm fine. I've been around your people for so long that I'm practically a human," she joked.

The brothers shared a nervous laugh, retaking their seats. "That's amazing. I thought I'd never see the day that a human and a fiend could live in peace with one another," Smith said.

Lara shrugged. "Not all of us are evil. Many of my kind are realizing that the only way for true peace is to adapt and share this world with the humans."

I cleared my throat, figuring it was now or never to inform them of my ambitious plan for the resistance. "We plan on recruiting both fiends and humans into this camp to fight the radical ones."

"What?! ... No way, it would never work," Ryan objected.

Smith placed a hand on his brother's shoulder. I already knew my plan would be met with opposition.

"We can rehabilitate them," Lara promised.

"You're sure of this? I mean, no offense, but they're monsters. They could turn on us at any time," Smith replied.

I couldn't help but laugh at this comment. Lara glanced over at me with a confused look.

"You said you know the story of my past, right?" I asked Ryan.

He nodded.

"Then you know that Captain Murphy was betrayed by Lieutenant Stark, which inevitably led to India Company's massacre in the Harush Forest."

The three of them were silent.

"What I'm trying to say is that fiend, human, or whatever—it doesn't matter. Anyone can turn on you at any time," I explained.

The two brothers nodded. I sent Lara a wink. She smirked. I knew I had sealed the deal.

Smith glanced from his brother to me before extending his hand. "We will follow you and your people to the end, Lance."

CHAPTER 7

Three days later we decided to conduct our first mission, hoping to find and kill an enemy patrol to gather weapons and ammunition. The flutter of butterflies in my stomach made my mouth dry. I kept the emotionless expression painted on my face, though, as the four of us put on our camouflage hunting gear and gloves, loaded a few magazines, and prepared ourselves mentally for the upcoming patrol.

Grant glanced over to me, a smile plastered to his face. I returned it, knowing he lived for this kind of action. "Game time," he called over with a wink.

I let out a nervous laugh, loading the magazine into my assault rifle and placing the weapon on safe. Ryan was off to the side watching. He had gotten stuck with babysitting Joshua. The disappointment was clear in his eyes.

"Cheer up, man. You're probably not even going to miss out on anything."

He rolled his eyes. "Yeah, right."

I shrugged. "There will be many more patrols to come."

With a grunt of agreement, he got up, nodded for Joshua to follow, and left the hut soon after.

"Bye. I will catch a big fish for you guys," Joshua called to us.

Lara smiled, giving him a wave good-bye. We had been blessed with good weather over the past few weeks, but it seemed that our luck was coming to an end as the sky filled with dark clouds rolling in from the south. Setting off for the patrol, we seemed to signal the wind, which threw the tree branches violently back and forth.

Fifteen minutes into the patrol, I raised my hand to signal a halt. We stopped and all huddled behind a huge boulder, taking shelter from the merciless wind while I dug around in my pocket and pulled out a map and compass.

"Maybe we should head back," Smith suggested.

Glancing from person to person, I could see that was what they wanted, but this mission was too important. Without any weapons or ammunition, we would bring nothing to the table for recruitment.

"We can't go back empty-handed," I muttered.

"But—" Smith said.

"No, we're continuing on with the mission," I said, trying my best to assert my authority. "Anyone else got anything to say?"

Grant and Lara shook their heads.

"Good," I muttered, returning my attention briefly to the map. "Let's go."

We emerged from the brush into a tiny clearing, cutting across toward Yorkshire Lake where Lara and I had stopped a few weeks before on our way back from South Lassetia. When I spotted troops in the surrounding tree line, I realized I had made the biggest mistake of my life.

"Lance, it's a trap!" Grant called to me in a panic.

I raised my hands. "I know. Put your weapons down, guys. It's over ... I'm sorry."

I placed my weapon on the ground in defeat and straightened up, squinting across the field at a couple of soldiers who appeared from the brush, heading our way. I glanced around the tree line, making out fifteen to twenty soldiers, all of whom had weapons trained on us.

Once they were within ten meters or so, three of them stopped, and their leader came forward. I decided to meet him halfway, hands raised slightly to show my compliance.

"I'm Lieutenant Jorgensen of the New World Order, and you are?"

"Lance ... Lance Andrew Burns. My friends and I are just passing through. We mean no harm to you and your men." I was trying to reason with him.

He smirked. "That's hard to believe when you stroll onto NWO territory with loaded assault rifles."

He motioned his men forward. This wasn't going to be good. I knew if we were taken prisoner, it would be over. The New World Order's torture methods were the worst in the war. "Whoa, whoa, whoa, boys ... Can't we work something out?" Grant called from behind.

Lieutenant Jorgensen gave me a devilish smirk. "I'm sure we can work something out at camp," he promised.

"Get your hands off me!" Lara's screams pierced my ears as the men began to bind her, Grant's and Smiths's hands behind their backs.

"*Calm down, Babe!*" I warned her through my thoughts.

"*You can't let them take me! They will find out I'm not human ... I'll be killed. Lance. Do something,*" her urgent plea came back.

"Okay, wait a second, wait a second. I'm a friend of Goss," I said desperately, playing my last card.

"Goss?" he replied.

I saw a spark of fear in Jorgensen's eyes. All it took was for me to give him a firm nod; he held his hand up to stop his men. "You mean captain Goss of the NWO?"

"Yes, we used to be in the resistance together. He would not be pleased with this treatment of an old friend," I warned him in an attempt to gain the upper hand.

Jorgensen bit his lip, glancing around at us. "Release them. If you're lying to me, so help me God, I will personally make sure your deaths are as long and painful as possible."

I nodded my thanks, relief fluttering into my stomach. I knew I had bought us some time.

Jorgensen's men took our weapons and then motioned us to follow them. Their camp wasn't far away. If we had kept going straight across the open field, we would have stumbled right into it, and that would have been far worse. As we entered the camp, I couldn't help noticing the amount of life. There had to be over a hundred soldiers and civilians taking shelter there. They had elaborate two-storey buildings, guard towers, and bunkers, indicating to me that this was a permanent base.

"Goss and his men are straight through there."

I followed Jorgensen's finger to a large official-looking hut in the distance. A soldier gave me a nudge with the barrel of his weapon. Having no choice, we briskly walked over and gave a knock on the door.

"Come in!" called a familiar voice.

I took a deep breath. My palms were sweating, making turning the doorknob almost impossible. As we entered the building, the blond man looked up from his work. A shocked expression spread over his face, allowing me to breathe a sigh of relief as he recognized me.

"Well, well, well, it's nice of you to drop in, Lance," he greeted us, each word laced with his rough Newfoundland accent.

I let out a nervous laugh. "Too bad we always got to meet like this," I said, nodding to one of his men who had us held at gunpoint.

Goss laughed, seeming to regain his composure, and with a wave of his hand had his soldiers lower their weapons. "Last I heard you boys ran into a little trouble in the Harush Forest. I thought you had been captured?"

"Can't always believe what you hear," I lied to him.

If he was to piece together what had happened the same way Ryan and Smith had, it would be game over for Lara. The New World Order had zero tolerance for fiends. "I suppose not," he grunted.

I watched as he rummaged around in his pocket and pulled out a package of smokes. "What up, buddy?" he called over to Grant with a smirk, appearing to have just remembered who he was.

"Long time no see," Grant replied civilly.

"So what brings you to my neck of the woods?" he asked, offering a smoke.

I waved the offer away, but Grant happily took one. "South Lassetia," I told him.

"Ah yes," he began, and took a puff of the cigarette. "There has been a lot of activity over there … That means you know something I don't."

Lara glanced over at me. I couldn't believe I had cornered myself like this. Usually I was better at working my way out of situations. The only thing left to do was break my number-one rule for interrogations and tell the truth.

"They have acquired a half blood."

"A what?" Goss asked.

"Half human and half fiend."

His eyes widened. "That's an abomination!"

I nodded my agreement. "They have the child locked up. Rumor has it that half-bloods carry within them amazing powers that could change this war. They're trying to harness those powers to use against us."

Goss put out his cigarette, tapping his fingers against the desk in thought. "The PLF no doubt wants this child for their own personal gain," he muttered to himself, more as a question than as a statement.

I nodded, while trying my best to hold back a smile in disbelief that he was buying my story. "We are not PLF anymore though," I added.

"Your allegiance died with Captain Murphy, huh?"

I shrugged. "We're starting up our own resistance around these parts."

"Hopefully not in the same footsteps as your predecessors," he joked.

I shook my head. "Our goal is the complete eradication of the fiends," I lied, taking a seat at his table and trying my best to play the part.

A smile spread across Goss's face. "It's about time you woke up, bi. what's your group called?"

I glanced around, not a clue what to say. "We're uh ... We are the RF."

"RF?"

"Yeah, the Revolutionary Force," I muttered, hoping he would believe it.

He poured two glasses of Scotch and handed me one. "To the RF?"

I nodded.

"To those who serve us," he muttered, holding it up.

"And to those who have fallen," I replied, tapping the drink against the table.

The Scotch was pretty harsh. I covered my mouth and let out a cough as he chuckled to himself. "Get it into you."

"So where do we go from here?" I asked him, trying to regain my composure.

He shrugged. "I'd like to offer you an alliance."

I glanced down at his hand held out to me.

"*Lance!*" Lara's voice objected in my head.

"*It's the only way we're getting out of here alive,*" I replied, silencing her.

I held my hand out to his and took a firm grasp. I hoped he couldn't feel the sweaty clamminess of it. Our eyes met, and he smiled, knowing the deal was done.

"Good to have you on board," he muttered, sitting back in his chair and lighting up another cigarette.

I grunted, sitting back as well and feeling like I had just sold my soul to the devil. The last thing I wanted was for him to embed men in my camp that could inform him about our activities.

"So are we free to go?" I asked, standing up and motioning for the others to do so as well.

He nodded. A look of disinterest had spread across his face.

"Where's Lieutenant Stark?" Grant asked him on our way out the door.

Goss's men glanced to the ground. This was clearly a taboo conversation around the camp. Goss took a long puff of the cigarette before answering. "You must kill a king to become a king."

"Let's go," I whispered, hurrying them out the door.

"Hey, Lance?" I turned around and spotted the sinister grin across his face. "I'll be seeing you real soon."

He held up his thumb and an index finger, forming a gun shape before pointing it at me. I returned it fearlessly, which seemed to catch him off guard.

"Unless we see you first," I called back and then made my exit.

"Just keep going," I whispered to them, hurrying them along. "Don't look at anyone."

We made our way briskly along the camp. I could practically feel the stares of the camp's residents burning through me.

"What about the guns?" Grant whispered.

"What's more important, the guns or your life?"

He shut up. As soon as we got to the outskirts of the camp, we broke into a dead sprint across the field and would not stop until we were two hundred meters away from where we had been captured.

"Great ... just great," Lara muttered.

I held up my hand, stopping the complaints before they came. "Don't worry about the weapons. I'll get them back tomorrow."

"It's not about the damn weapons," Lara argued, placing her hands on her hips to catch her breath. "We just signed a deal with the devil. The NWO are cold-blooded killers, Lance."

The rest all grunted in agreement. I sighed. All I could do was shrug. "We'll deal with it when the time comes."

I gave them all the next day off to do construction

around the camp or whatever they felt like. Lying in the HQ hut, I watched the dull morning rays peak through the cracks of the walls as the songs of birds began to play outside. I tried to get dressed in silence, but the dull snores of Lara came to a halt.

She stirred and opened her eyes, a warm smile spreading across her face. "Morning, sweetie," she whispered.

"Good morning, Babe."

She motioned me to her. I gave her a kiss, bringing the blanket back up to her neck. "Go to sleep. I need to get some things done."

She stared at me curiously. "You're going back?" she asked.

I nodded and returned my attention to getting dressed. "I have no choice. We need those weapons."

"Be careful," she urged.

"Always am," I whispered with and placed a kiss on her cheek before taking my leave of the hut.

The hike back to the NWO camp felt surreal, it hadn't been that long ago that Goss and I had been friends, one day that all changed though when our camp had a mutiny forming the new world order leaving us, the surviving members of the peoples liberation force to flee to our eventual demise. I was greeted at the entrance of the NWO's camp by a guard. Goss was summoned, appearing a short time later. "What's up, bi?" he asked.

"We forgot some of our possessions here yesterday," I explained.

Goss chuckled to himself, waving me through. I followed him along the long, winding path and maze of wooden huts toward his HQ hut. Camp life was dead, with not a soul wandering around. All that was left from the night before were smouldering ashes periodically shooting small gray shrouds of smoke into the air.

"Big party last night," he said, answering my stares.

"What's to celebrate?" I grunted.

"Being alive, of course."

I laughed to myself, climbing the small flight of wooden steps to the hut. He opened the door, revealing our four assault rifles lying in the corner. "Noticed you guys were pretty low on ammo. So there are four vests with ten mags each. And a backpack filled with some goodies," he told me.

I spotted them, becoming more at ease. If he was supplying us with ammunition, it meant we had at least earned his trust.

"Thank you, Goss. You don't know how much this means to me," I said, giving his hand a firm shake.

"I feel like we got off on the wrong foot last night. I hope our past won't affect the future," he told me.

I nodded in agreement. "We just didn't know what to expect," I told him.

He laughed. "I'm still the same guy, and let's not forget, if it wasn't for me, you wouldn't even be alive today."

"I know," I muttered, gathering up the weapons and giving him another firm shake of the hand.

"What's your grid?" he asked as I headed out the door.

I cursed under my breath, wishing I could have got away without telling him. "0845, 9876."

He smiled, jotting it down. "All right. Well, we will be in touch soon enough, I imagine."

"Sounds good," I lied.

I left the hut, made my way back down the path to the main gate, and got waved through by the guard. Less than an hour later, I was back in the safety of our camp.

Setting the weapons down in our headquarters hut, I glanced over at Lara and Joshua. They were both still asleep, their snores mingling into one. I chuckled to myself, closed the door, and went back outside. Grant was up, collecting some firewood. I could hear the snores of Smith and Ryan in the distance. All in all, it was going to be a lazy day. That's all I wanted though. They needed a break to recharge their batteries as much as I did. Grant spotted me and came over with a cup of coffee, probably salvaged from a ration bag.

"Sup?" he asked, offering me the coffee.

I accepted his offer and took a sip, the taste instantly tickling my taste buds. I let out a sigh of relief, giving him a thankful nod. "Got the weapons back."

I handed the coffee back to him, and he took a seat on a log, glancing back up to me as I rummaged around in the backpack Goss had given me.

"I saw that," he said, taking another sip of his coffee before asking, "So is Goss a friend or a foe?"

All I could offer was a confused shrug. "Time will tell, I guess."

I paused. My heart was skipping a few beats as I came across the contents at the bottom of the bag.

"Bingo," I whispered.

Grant leaned over my shoulder, his eyes lighting up with delight as I pushed aside a tarp revealing grenades and C-4 at the bottom of the bag. He laughed, offering me another sip of the coffee. I waved it away. "You enjoy that coffee. I'm going to go sit by the ocean for a little while."

"You okay?"

I nodded. "Just want some time to myself. That's all."

I headed down the path, glimpsing the blue sea in the distance through breaks in the vegetation. Arriving at the edge of the cliff, I took a seat and let the gentle ocean breeze beat against my body, together with the rays of the morning sun. A seagull flew by, gliding with expanded wings on a thermal. Not a care in the world ... pure freedom.

"Morning, sexy," Lara's voice called from behind me not long after.

I glanced back, heard the rustle of the brush from the direction in which she was approaching, and smiled as she took a seat beside me. "Morning." I greeted her with a kiss.

She giggled, her attention then turning to the vast ocean in front of us. "It's beautiful."

I nodded. "To think I would have missed all this if you hadn't saved me."

She cuddled, giving me another kiss. I returned it, a content feeling flowing through me. Her hands were clammy cold. Glancing down, I spotted her bare white knuckles.

It was time for her to feed. I knew she just didn't want to ask. "Have some blood," I told her, rolling up the sleeve of my hunting shirt.

She stared at my arm before her and then tore her eyes away. "I can in a few days. My cravings aren't that bad yet," she offered.

I shook my head. "Just do it. I hate seeing you like this, Babe."

She placed her hands on my wrist to keep it steady. "I'll be gentle."

She flashed me a warm smile, which I returned before closing my eyes. The familiar searing pain of her dagger-like teeth piercing my arm soon followed. As they tore my skin and muscles, my arm turned warm, and blood started gushing from the wound.

My eyes snapped open as I heard a rustling in the bushes behind us. Lara's eyes opened too. We saw Joshua wandering out from the tree line, humming a hymn to himself with a smile as warm as the sun lighting up his face. Then he saw us. Stopping in his tracks, he glanced from my arm to Lara's bloodstained face. Her eyes returned to normal, fangs disappearing, but it was too late.

"Aghh!" he screamed and took off, running back down toward the camp.

"Joshua!" Lara called after him.

She quickly healed my arm, and then we chased after him. Entering the camp and gasping for air, we found Grant struggling to keep the flailing child pinned to the ground. "No! ... Don't kill me, please don't kill me!" Joshua screamed as Lara and I approached.

We held our hands up to the child in a nonthreatening manner, taking a knee by his side. "Calm down, Joshua. It's okay. Look ... my arm's fine," I told him, showing the unscathed place where Lara had been feeding.

"She's a monster, Grant. Please save me," he begged, ignoring me and looking up at Grant for support.

Grant sent him a reassuring smile, glancing at us. "He's seen, huh?"

Lara and I nodded.

"Listen, buddy, not all fiends are bad. There are good ones too," he tried to explain.

Joshua glanced over at Lara in fear. "But fiends killed my mommy."

I glanced over at Ryan and Smith, who had come out from their shelter, rubbing sleep from their eyes. "What the heck is going on?"

"Nothing," I called over in annoyance, waving them away.

Lara tried to send Joshua a warm smile and reached out to pat his face in reassurance. He recoiled in fear. I could see the hurt in her eyes.

"You don't need to be scared, Joshua. I'm a good fiend."

"Can I let you go?" Grant asked him.

He nodded, got up, and wiped the dirt off his pants before staring at us in fear. I let out a discouraged sigh, glancing over at Lara. We would have to start all over again now to regain his trust.

Joshua shifted nervously before asking, "You're not going to hurt me?" His voice was still quivering.

Lara shook her head.

"Pinky-swear?" he asked.

Lara knelt down, offering him her pinky. He wrapped his around hers.

"I will never hurt you, Joshua," she said and placed a light kiss on his forehead.

He backed away, glancing up at Grant.

"You hungry?" Grant asked.

Joshua gave him an uncertain nod. Grant smiled, giving his back a pat. He seemed to put his best foot forward at rekindling the child's trust.

"Go grab something out of the hut, buddy. I'll be in shortly."

The boy walked away and vanished behind the door of the hut, sending us one last fearful look.

"It would probably be for the best if you didn't spend time with him for a bit," I muttered to Lara.

"But—" she began to protest.

I held up my hand.

"I can take care of him for a little while," Grant offered.

The three of us came to the agreement that his idea

would be the best. Lara let out a disappointed sigh as Grant went into the hut to check on Joshua.

"It will be fine, Babe. He knows you're his friend," I tried to reassure her.

She glanced up at me. Tears were forming in her eyes as her lip began quivering. "I'm so stupid. I should have known he would follow me."

I shook my head, trying to reason with her. "He was going to find out sooner or later."

"I suppose so," she muttered. "Can I go see him?"

I shook my head. "Just give it some time."

Entering to the hut, I was greeted by the sight of Grant and Joshua sharing a can of pears.

"Feeling better, buddy?" I asked Joshua, placing a hand on his knee and squatting down beside him.

He glanced up at me before giving a nod.

I smiled. "Lara misses you. Do you want to talk to her?"

He nodded. I helped him up, and he followed me out the door. Lara was outside, pacing back and forth like a mother whose son had just been admitted into the hospital.

"Joshua!" she exclaimed, arms wide open.

He gave her a hug. "I'm sorry," he whispered.

She patted his back, tears trickling down her face. "Oh, it's okay, hon. I'm sorry that you found out this way. I'll never let the fiends get you."

I saw a glimmer of excitement in his eyes.

"Can you turn into a big one?" he asked her, holding his arms as wide as they would go.

She laughed, giving him a nod. "Would you like to see?"

He nodded his head furiously. Lara smiled and began to take her clothes off.

"Are you sure this is a good idea?" I asked her through our telepathic communication.

"Yes, it will be fine. I have my fiend's wild side under control." She handed me her clothes.

Before I could object, her muscles began to go into spasms as the transformation commenced. Joshua took a few steps back, his eyes widened, and then just like that, she had turned into the massive creature of a fiend. She let out a gut-wrenching roar, bringing Grant, Ryan, and Smith barrelling from their shelters, guns raised and ready for a fight.

Waving to them that it was fine, I couldn't help laughing to myself. Lara bowed her gigantic head toward Joshua, lay down on the ground, and rolled over. Joshua clapped his hands in excitement.

Unable to hold back a smile by the sight of the young boy's joy, I approached Lara's side and ran my hand along her belly. The soft fur sifted through my fingers as she purred to herself peacefully.

"Would you like to give her a pat?" I offered Joshua.

Before I had finished the sentence, he was by my side, patting her in excitement. "It's just like a big doggy!" he exclaimed.

I nodded, reminding him to be gentle as Lara rolled back over. The massive claws retreated into her paw as she began to play fight with him.

"Careful, Lara!"

"I know, I know," her thoughts came floating back to my head.

"Want to go for a ride?" I asked.

Joshua nodded.

I grabbed his waist and hoisted him up onto her back. She got up on all fours and walked around the camp.

71

"Whoa," he called out as she playfully tried to shake him off.

"*Want to go to the lake?*" she asked me.

"*Sure.*"

While she played around with Joshua, I went into the hut, grabbed an assault rifle, and filled a backpack with our picnic blanket, her clothes, and something to snack on.

"What's up?" Grant asked.

"Lara and I are going to have a play day down at the lake with him," I called back.

"Cool," he muttered.

I glanced over as he stared at the ground in thought. I could tell something was wrong.

"What're your plans for the day?" I asked.

He shrugged. "I'll probably go fishing with the brothers," he replied, referring to Smith and Ryan.

Grant took a seat, pulled out his hunting knife, and started to sharpen it in boredom.

"Is there something wrong?" I asked.

He glanced up at me before returning his attention to the knife. "I don't know. It just seems like you and Lara are getting pretty close with that kid."

I shrugged. "He just lost his parents."

"We can't guarantee his safety," Grant muttered.

"I know."

He nodded and then went silent. I left, ignoring his warnings.

"Get on, Lance!" Joshua called.

Lara knelt down so I could hoist myself onto her back.

The flight to the lake was gentle. I held on to Lara's neck, with Joshua, who was staring at the distant mountains, in front of me.

"Look," I called to him with a tap on the shoulder. His eyes followed my finger down to a meadow where a moose and its calf were grazing.

"Cool!" he exclaimed.

Lara began her decent as the lake appeared in the distance.

"End of the line," I said as we hit the ground. We jumped off her back, and she transformed back into her human form, sharing the same smile as Joshua.

"Did you have fun?" she asked hopefully.

He nodded and gave her a hug. "Thank you, Lara!"

I gave her the clothes back. Then we set up the picnic and ate in silence as the gentle breeze blew against the lake. Once we were done, Joshua got up, wiped the sand off his pants, jogged down to the lake, and went for a swim.

"He's cute," Lara whispered as we watched him swim around in the shallows.

"Yeah, too bad he will never have a family to share his life with," I muttered.

She glanced over at me. "We could be his family."

I laughed to myself. "We're on the verge of going to war, Babe. How are we going to take care of him?"

She was silent, and her attention shifted back to the lake. "He and Rashellia would be so cute together," she whispered to herself.

I didn't say anything. So she got up moodily, dug around in the backpack, and pulled out a bar of soap.

"I hate how you're always so serious. Why can't you just enjoy the beautiful day, Lance?" And without giving me time to answer, she stormed down the beach to Joshua. "Hey, buddy?" I heard her call.

I let out a disgruntled sigh and leaned back on the

blanket, closing my eyes and letting the soft rays of the sun bounce off me. When I reopened them, it was to the sight of Lara and Joshua washing themselves in the shallows. I put on a fake smile, got up, and jogged down to the shoreline.

Wanting to relax and enjoy the day, I tried my best to shoo my worries away, but there was just too much on my mind to ignore. It seemed that whenever things were going my way, someone I loved died. So I always had to be alert, knowing all too well what being complacent with our situation would lead to.

"It's about time, grumpy pants," Lara called playfully as I waded out to them. The fresh waves felt so nice, lapping against my body.

Letting out a laugh, I splashed them, which sparked a water fight. We spent the rest of the day fooling around in the water before Lara flew us back to camp.

As we arrived, I spotted Grant waiting for us. His body language told me that something had happened.

"What is it?" I asked as soon as we landed.

"We found Fiona washed up on the shoreline. She wants to see you," he explained.

"Is she all right?"

He shook his head. "Some sort of war started down there. She's been hurt pretty bad. Ryan and Smith are doing their best to take care of her."

Without hesitation, I jumped back onto Lara's back and handed Joshua down to Grant.

"*Let's go!*" I shouted through my thoughts. She took off, streaking toward the ocean.

It didn't look good as we landed at the beach. I ran over to Ryan and Smith, who were kneeling over Fiona's body.

She had long gashes across her body. Lara began to work on her immediately.

"What happened?" I asked.

Fiona spat out a mouthful of blood before explaining. "The war has started for control of the sea. I was visiting my father when the Nordics came in and began killing everyone. I barely escaped with my life."

"Your father?" I asked.

She shook her head. "He was killed."

I watched in fear as a violent tremor coursed through her body. She gripped my hand, her web-like fingers feeling odd against mine.

"You're going to be fine. Just stay calm," I whispered.

"She has internal bleeding, These wounds will take days for me to heal completely." Lara's thoughts came flooding in.

"Just stabilize her. We need to take her to a more secure location."

Lara began casting spells. Blue, green, and red lights traveled along Fiona's body like caterpillars, coming to rest at each wound fading into the skin. Fiona's breathing slowed. Her grasp on my hand loosened, and she whispered her thanks to us.

"Don't move. The comfort is only temporary," Lara warned.

We found two sturdy logs and rolled one to each end of the blanket, forming a stretcher. Lara and I lay Fiona on it. Then Ryan and Smith each picked up an end and followed us through the shallows. A few minutes later, we discovered a small cove and placed Fiona in the shallow end where she could rest on a sandbar. She seemed content for the moment.

"You're leaving?" she asked, opening up an eye.

I nodded. "I will be back. Lara's staying for now."

She waved her hand with a laugh. "I'm fine. Don't worry yourselves about me. I just need time to rest."

So Smith, Ryan, and I waded through the shallows of the shoreline back to the beach and made the hike up the cliff back to camp.

"What is that creature?" Smith asked once we were in the privacy of the headquarters hut.

"She is a Shellian. They came from the same planet as the fiends. Her name is Fiona. She is the last pureblood of her race."

"So they're our allies?" Ryan asked.

I couldn't help a smirk. "That's where it gets tricky."

"Huh?" he replied.

"The Shellians are just as evil as the fiends. Their only goal is world domination. They made a pact on Fraturna to an alliance with the fiends but then turned on them by making the same deal with the relics, who were rising to power. The fiends, not having enough numbers on their side, were inevitably defeated and fled to Earth to rebuild their lives. I can only assume that the relics then turned on the Shellians, and that is why they are both here now."

"Why should we trust this one, then?"

I shrugged. There was no real way to know whether Fiona would ever side her people with us, but she had saved my life. The least I could do was return the favor. "What choice do we have?" I finally asked.

Before the brothers could reply, a rustling outside shifted our attention to the hut entrance. Grant emerged through the front door.

"Is she all right?"

"Lara has her stabilized," I answered. "I'm going down

to guard her for the night. Send someone else down to relieve me at midnight."

Once everyone had agreed to the plan, I grabbed my assault rifle and left. As I arrived back at the sandbar, Lara and Fiona were talking in a hushed whisper.

"Feeling better?" I asked, sitting down in the shallow water beside them.

"I'll feel better when my people have been avenged," Fiona said. She glanced over at Lara. "May I have some time alone with Lance?"

Lara looked at me, and I gave her a nod. Without a word, she gave Fiona a hug, transformed, and flew back to camp. Silence enveloped Fiona and me as the waves gently lapped against our bodies.

"Remember when you said you would do anything to repay me?" she asked.

I gulped and nodded, glancing over at her.

"I need your help now," she said, staring out to the sea almost as if in a trance.

"What do you need me to do?"

She let out a sigh, a tear trickling down her face. "Go to war with the Nordics."

There was a pause. I don't think she realized what an insane idea it was.

"I and my three-man army?" I asked. The sarcasm in my voice was unmistakeable. I knew she wouldn't like my comment, but it had to be said. "We have a war going on up here, Fiona. I can't just go to war with everyone."

She scowled at me, raising her hand for silence. It worked; I fell silent. She returned her attention out to the ocean, biting her lip in thought. "We have special-force weapons that can be fired underwater. The Russians used them on us when they first discovered our presence. We cannot use them," she went on, holding up her webbed hand to illustrate her point, "But your people can. The four of you would be integrated with the survivors of my tribe and go to war with the Nordics. Once I gain the support of the people, and expose Faroqua, the leader of the terrorist faction for who he is, I'll be able to take it from there."

I grinded my teeth, knowing it was going to be no easy task. "What do I get out of this?"

"What you've always wanted," Fiona replied.

"Huh?"

"Your daughter."

I looked at her in disbelief. A sly smile spread across her pale lips. "The river that flows by South Lassetia leads to the ocean. If you help us, we will help you get your daughter back."

An offer like that was impossible to refuse, no matter what the cost. I held out my hand to her. All I could do was hope that she would keep her end of the bargain. Her soft, webby fingers wrapped around mine in a tight squeeze. Our eyes met.

"You have a deal, my lady."

Fiona's smile faded. "Good," she muttered. "Very good."

I watched the setting sun. My thoughts were filled with the idea that if we made it out of this new contest alive, I would be that much closer to having Rashellia back in my arms.

CHAPTER 8

It took two full weeks for Fiona's wounds to recover, but once she was back to full strength, her only concern was going to war with the Nordic Shellians. We had decided that Lara would stay behind with Joshua since the Shellians probably wouldn't accept her help anyway. I, Grant, Ryan, and Smith were huddled around a diagram of Fiona's village she had drawn into the sand.

"When do you think she will be back?" Ryan asked.

I shrugged. Fiona had left a few hours before to find her servants, who were hiding in an underwater cavern not far from the beach. Out of the corner of my eye, just as I was tearing my gaze away, I spotted the Shellians surfacing from the depths led by Fiona.

"Greetings," she called to us as they waded through the rocky surface.

I chuckled to myself. Her speech was always so formal. "What's up?" I asked, offering her my hand to help her up onto the beach.

She accepted it and with a smirk on her face, said sarcastically, "The sky."

We all laughed, her humor breaking the tension as our unlikely allies introduced themselves to us.

"My name is Duraturo, commander of the Atlantic army," a strong, well-built six-foot Shellian introduced himself, giving each of our hands a shake.

The cool clammy feeling of his touch felt weird. Not thinking, I wiped my hand off on my pants. He noticed it. I could tell he was not impressed as he whispered something in Fiona's ear.

She patted his chest, giving him a nod of her head to let it go. He glared at me. "Stupid humans," he muttered under his breath before leaving back into the surf.

"Cheery fellow," Grant said.

Smith, Ryan, and I couldn't help laughing. I glanced over at Fiona; her expression was neutral. "I'm sorry about Duraturo's hospitality," she said.

I waved it away. "It's fine. I don't want to get off on the wrong foot. We are here to make friends not enemies," I said, returning the apology.

She nodded her agreement. Then a few more of her guards introduced themselves. I glanced back to the surface as another Shellian emerged from the depths. This one was a female, her long silver-white hair draping down her back. "This is my sister Ysolda," she introduced us as the Shellian came to her side.

We gave our introductions politely. Ryan had obviously been struck by her beauty, having not taken his eyes off her since she arrived. I saw her catch him. He shared a shy smile with her, ripping his attention away.

Ysolda whispered something into her sister's ear. Then the two shared a giggle among themselves.

"So where are the weapons at?" I asked, noticing that

they were only armed with sling shots, bows, arrows, and a dagger, which hung off their belts.

"They are in my father's city."

I glanced at Fiona in disbelief. "You mean the city that was taken over?"

She nodded. This wasn't part of the deal. She had promised me we would be supplied with weaponry.

"Well, looks like there's no time to waste, then," Ryan spoke up.

I stared at him in disbelief. I had practically had to drag him down to the beach that morning, listening to the complaints of how this wasn't our war to fight. Now, because of some hot Shellian, he was ready to charge face-first into an army. "Okay ... just ignore him ... This wasn't the agreement," I told Fiona.

I could see the look of concern on her face. "I'm sorry that I misled you, Lance, but you would do the same for your people. We will supply you with our traditional weaponry and then assault the city and gain access to the weapons as promised."

With a sigh, I glanced at the three of them. "Can I have a few minutes with my men?" I asked her.

She nodded, and the two of them went into the surf, followed by their body guards, as we headed up the beech and took a seat under the protection of the cliff.

"So what do you guys think?" I asked, wanting their opinion.

"I say live to fight another day," Grant grunted.

"We need to help them. If they are sincere on their promise to help us against the fiends, then we will be able to start taking the fight to them and maybe even get your daughter back," Ryan objected.

"I'm with my brother," Smith muttered.

I glanced back to Grant. He shrugged with a smirk on his face. "I'll follow you anywhere, bro. You know that."

"Let's do this, then," I told them.

We got up, went down to the ocean, and were greeted at the surface by Fiona and her sister. "We'll do it," I told her.

"Excellent ... You've made the right choice, Lance."

Fiona gave Grant a kiss, allowing him to breath underwater. Her sister then gave Smith a kiss. I was next in line for Ysolda when Ryan got in front of me. I laughed, giving him a playful shove before receiving the kiss from Fiona.

The effects of her power instantly took effect, making the air hard to breath. I fell into the water, relieved by being able to breathe normal again. "You guys can talk normal under here," I told my guys. It was their first time.

"Cool," Grant called, jumping around on the ocean floor. "Feels like we're on the moon," he added.

Fiona let us fool around for a little while, casting individual spells on us to acclimatize us to the ocean's temperature, making our skin more durable to deal with walking on the ocean floor, and stuff like that. "All these fish around, and it takes all day just to get one," I muttered to myself as we began walking along the rocky surface toward Fiona's village.

Fiona must have heard me. She slowed down and fell back to my side. "You're having trouble supplying food for your camp, Lance?"

I shook my head. "We will in the future though, as we gain more recruits," I told her.

"We could help," she offered.

"Let's see if we make it through this first," I replied.

She laughed, nodding in agreement. I glanced ahead at Ryan and Ysolda. She was pointing out underwater caves and fish and rambling onto him about Shellian lifestyle. He would in turn tell her what life on Earth was like.

"I smell love in the air," I whispered to Fiona, nodding ahead to her sister.

Fiona laughed, shaking her head. "Ysolda wouldn't be foolish enough to fall in love with an Earth dweller. My father would never allow it." She paused. I guess she had just realized she was now in charge.

"Would you allow it?"

She stopped, glancing over at me. Her face scrunched up as she looked at the two of them. "I don't know," she finally muttered, kicking a rock along as we resumed walking to her village.

"Your people are going to want to know your stand on things like that," I told her. "You're either going to walk in your father's footsteps or build a new path for yourself."

"I know," she replied.

The Shellian village began to appear in the distance. Clumps of mud, forming igloo-like shapes beside one another, were lined up with a mixture of mud-and-rock walls separating them. "Greetings, Your Highness," one of the guards said, taking a knee as we approached.

She gave him a nod, motioning for him to get up. He obediently did so, returning to standing guard as we entered the village.

"Where is everyone?" I asked as we walked along the deserted village.

"I ordered them to flee until the war with the Nordics is over."

"It's for the best though," I told her.

She nodded in agreement. I couldn't help but be a little relieved by her decision. It meant that she was compassionate, a trait her father lacked.

"So where's the party at?" Grant asked once we came to a halt by a few stones to sit on.

We laughed, but the Shellians didn't. They glanced at one another with a confused look. "Party?" Ysolda asked.

"Like to relax, eat, sing, joke around, dance, get drunk, stuff like that," Ryan explained to her.

She blushed. I could tell the concept was foreign to them. "We don't party very much," Fiona replied.

I laughed. "He was joking. We have a war to fight; we can party after."

Fiona gave a nervous laugh, not seeming very open to the idea. "If we win, we will have a party with your people," she said, glancing over at her sister hesitantly.

Duraturo appeared from the cave above where Fiona lived, and came down with bows and quivers, filled with arrows and slung around his shoulder.

"Great," Grant muttered.

"Would you four please line up," Duraturo instructed.

We did so while Fiona and Ysolda grabbed the bow and arrows and handed them individually out to us.

"Who here knows how to use these?" Duraturo asked.

The four of us stood in silence. All the Shellians laughed. "That was to be expected. You Earth dwellers always rely on your high-tech gear … That is okay though. We have plenty of time to train," Duraturo called to us while setting up a target about twenty-five meters away.

"Who's first?" Ysolda asked.

Ryan raised his hand, going over to her. She smiled

warmly as he approached and unshouldered his bow. "Please gather in," she called to us.

We did; she handed him an arrow. "Do you see this notch?" she asked us, holding up another arrow.

We nodded. The arrows had no tails on them. I could only assume because they weren't necessary underwater. She lined up the notch with the string of her bow and then pulled back as far as it would go.

"Okay, now watch. The farther I pull it back, the more power that will be in the shot. To aim, look slightly over the arrow. Close your left or right eye, depending on what hand you use, and then let go."

She let it go, and the arrow took off and hit its target dead center, leaving nothing but a trail of bubbles in its wake. "Tada, it's as simple as that," she said.

Ryan armed his arrow on the bow, took aim, and then pulled it back. "Nice and straight," Ysolda corrected him.

She placed her arm on his lower back, straightened him up, and then whispered something into his ear. Whatever encouragement she gave him did not work. He let go, and the arrow went flying way off to the left.

We all laughed. It turned out we should have held our tongues as we each stepped up and missed equally bad. "Watch and learn, ladies," I called back on my second attempt.

I pulled the arrow back and then let go. It pitifully wobbled out of the bow and landed three or four feet in front of me. "It's going to be a long day," I overheard Duraturo mutter on my way back to the group.

His prediction wasn't far off either. The only two with any success were Grant and Ryan, who would get a fluke shot every now and then, hitting the edge of the target.

As dusk began to set in, we decided to call it quits. Some Shellian hunters had returned with fish for us to eat.

We watched in disgust as they bit into their meals, devouring a full fish raw. "Is something wrong?" Ysolda asked Ryan as we watched.

"You don't cook this?" he asked her.

She shrugged. "Why waste time?"

"Our bodies can't handle eating these raw. They carry bacteria and stuff," Ryan explained.

"Aw. Yes, I have forgotten about that," she replied.

She left momentarily to talk to her sister in the distance. Fiona nodded, and Ysolda returned, motioning us up to the cave. "My sister and I will cook your meals. Please follow me."

We did following her up the rocky path to the cave. She wiped her feet off on the seaweed, and we followed suit politely. Fiona was already waiting for us up there. "Hold your breath," she instructed.

She whispered something under her breath to herself, and her hair began to float back and forth with the flow of the current. She opened her eyes; the dull green glow illuminated the small cave. "Shiato," she said.

I was almost thrown off my feet as the water was ripped out of the cave, forming a glass-like mirror at the foot of it. My lungs burned as I gasped in a fresh breath of air. They quickly kissed us, allowing us to breath normally again.

"I didn't know Shellians used magic," Grant muttered to me.

I nodded. "They can transform too."

He glanced at me in disbelief. "Really?"

"Yep, when I first met Fiona, she was in her Shellian transformation form. It's a dragon-eel-looking thing—" I was cut off by Fiona as she and her sister busily combined their powers to build a fire.

"We call it Kimoatio," she told us.

"What?" I asked.

"The transformation," she explained. "Kimoatio was the saviour of our people in the first war between us and the fiends. He alone killed thousands. He learned the voice of Kwan to give him the powers of transformation. My family is the last of his bloodline. We are the only ones who can call upon the spirit of Kimoatio to help us in battle."

I watched a blue gel-like substance come from Ysolda's fingertip as she formed a circle on the rock surface of the cave. With a snap of Fiona's finger, a flame came out. The blue gel that Ysolda had cast ignited, forming the fire.

"How long will that burn?" Smith asked.

"Forever," Ysolda replied.

"Damn, we need you guys up in our camp," Grant muttered.

We all laughed. I personally couldn't even think of a time where it wasn't a struggle to get the fire going. Fiona retrieved a rack they had built, placed it over the fire, and then set the fish on top.

Fiona and the others were extremely accommodating, probably gracious for our help. They made us each a bed out of some sort of ocean moss, which was surprisingly comfortable to fall asleep on. It wasn't long after we had fallen asleep when I was shaken awake by Fiona.

"What is it?" I asked.

She brought her finger to her lips, motioning toward the entrance of the cave. I followed her to the edge, lay flat against the rocky surface, and spotted two Shellians, searching the village below. "Scouts?" I asked.

She nodded and gave me a kiss, allowing me to breathe underwater. I followed her down within range of the scouts and drew my bow. "On my mark," she whispered, arming an arrow before drawing the string back.

I armed my arrow, waiting for her shot. As the pair came into view, there was a sharp hiss from her bow. The bow had snapped, causing the arrow to sail through the air and hit its target straight in the neck. The Shellian collapsed to the ground and clutched his neck in agony as purplish blood filled the water around us.

I shot my arrow and hit the other in the lower abdomen. He let out a cry of pain, falling to the ground. Fiona quickly ran from our cover, slit his throat, and stabbed him multiple times.

"He's dead, Fiona," I grunted, grabbing a hold of her arm.

She paused, glancing back to me before giving the dead Shellian one more vicious stab to the throat. "They would show my people no mercy. So why should we?"

I gave her a shrug, knowing the best thing to do was to remain silent. "We need to wake the others; we can no longer stay here. The Nordics will know something has happened once their scouts don't return."

Half an hour later, we were all up heading north, away from Fiona's village, toward her father's army, which had a stronghold about three days away. We were accompanied by about twenty or so Shellian hunters and five guards. Ysolda and Ryan were leading the way. I couldn't help smiling to myself. They reminded me of when Lara and I had fallen in love.

"Awesome," Ryan exclaimed as a group of dolphins swam by.

Ysolda followed his finger to the dolphins above and then whispered something into his ear. He nodded. She let out a song-like call. The dolphins looped around to us and began circling.

Ysolda held out her hand. One of them swam down and came to a rest in her arms. She gently petted its head and motioned Ryan forward. He did, happily petting it before it swam away, doing a flip out of the surface above.

Fiona called another one down and let the others pet its head. Its skin felt like soft rubber to my touch. As night approached, we found a small cave to rest in. Fiona built a fire, and the others went to bed. I pretended to be asleep, listening to Ryan and Ysolda flirting with one another.

"How are your feet?" she whispered to him as they cuddled under the light of the flickering fire.

"Sore."

I peeked over at them. She began massaging his feet. Fiona was watching from across the cave as well. "Thank you," Ryan whispered.

She nodded with an affectionate twinkle in her eyes. "It's no problem. I know you'd do the same for me."

Ysolda glanced over to her sister and then leaned forward. She and Ryan met each other halfway for a kiss. Fiona sat there, staring at the pair with a solemn expression across her face. Ryan wrapped his arm around her, cuddling affectionately.

The snores of the pair soon filled the water. Fiona continued to stare at them in shock. I laughed to myself, leaned back, and let sleep overcome me, knowing tomorrow's events would be nothing short of interesting.

CHAPTER 9

I was one of the first to wake up the next morning. Fiona was outside the cave, sitting on a rock and chewing on a plant deep in thought. "Morning," I greeted her, taking a seat on the rock.

She glanced over to me and then back to the marine life in front of us. "Good morning, Lance."

"What will you do to them?" I asked, nodding toward Ryan and Ysolda.

"Nothing," she replied, taking me by surprise.

Fiona let out a sigh, her attention shifting back to me. "I have realized that there is no sense looking for love, Lance. Love will find you. I am not sure why it has found Ysolda in the form of that Earth dweller, but I'm sure there is a reason. Who am I to interfere?"

I grunted my agreement. I was glad that she and I saw eye to eye on this topic. "When I first met Lara, I thought it could never work between a fiend and a human, but it did. I'm sure it will for your sister as well," I told her.

Fiona nodded, offering me the root of the plant she was chewing on. I laughed, shooing the offer away with my hand. "We should probably wake the troops up," I suggested.

She took another bite from the plant and nodded her agreement. It took our group three more days to reach Lord Olaf's army. When we did, it was not the welcome party I was expecting.

As we crossed an open field toward a labyrinth of underwater caves, twenty to thirty armed Shellians appeared around the rocky outskirts, staring down at us, bows at the ready with arrows loaded. Duraturo raised his hand to us, his webbed fingers expanding, motioning for us to put our weapons down. He called out something in their foreign tongue to the Shellians around us.

There was no answer. Five agonizing minutes past by before a Shellian, who appeared to be in a senior position, came toward us with an entourage of guards. "Duraturo!" he called out to us.

The two men met each other halfway and shook hands. Smiles and laughs soon followed as they talked among themselves, relieving the tension that had only moments before plagued the air around us. "Fiona," Duaturo called back to us.

We all took a knee as she passed. The Shellian talking to Duraturo bowed his head. "Greetings, my lady," he said politely.

She returned the gesture with a diplomatic smile on her face. "Lusion, this is Fiona, Queen of the Atlantic Region," Duraturo introduced them.

"Pleasure to make your acquaintance, Your Highness."

"Likewise," she replied.

She motioned her sister to come. "Aw, Princess Ysolda.

It's good to see you again, my dear," Lusion greeted her with a kiss on the cheek.

"You've heard of my father's death?" Fiona asked him.

He nodded. "Most unfortunate news."

Fiona nodded her agreement. "We have much to talk about, commander."

He glanced over to me before voicing his agreement. "Right, this is not an appropriate time or place though. Please, may you and your people accompany my men to our base?"

She nodded, motioning for us to follow. Once we were settled in an empty cave, Lusion summoned Duraturo, Fiona, and Ysolda to his place. "Lance would you care to join us?" Fiona asked.

"Huh?" Lusion asked her, confused. "What business does an Earth dweller have with our war against the Nordics?"

"This Earth dweller saved my life. He is one of us," Fiona assured him.

Lusion eyed me down as I joined Fiona and Ysolda. He shifted around in place. I could tell my presence bothered him, but in the end he bowed his head, saying, "Yes, my lady."

We followed him through a maze of tunnels along the underwater cavern until we came to a rest in a dug-out den. Seaweed clung from the ceiling, dangling in front. There was a bed of moss in a corner, and a few flat stones, which I presumed served as seats. He motioned for us to sit down.

"I'm saddened by the news of your father's fate. He was a good man. I'd follow him into the depths of Jaden Hall," he began. "However, I know what you have come to ask of me, and I cannot do it."

"What is it you think I have come to ask you?" Fiona asked.

"To retake your father's stronghold."

Everyone went silent. "You will do as the Queen asks," Duraturo spoke up with anger in each word.

Lusion shook his head. "I will not sacrifice my men on a suicide mission. The Nordics' army is spanning out across this entire region. We need all the forces we can muster up to protect our homeland."

"You vowed to protect the Kimoatio bloodline. You cannot abandon us at our weakest moment," Duraturo growled.

"I vowed to protect Lord Olaf, which I have done time and time again. He is no longer alive. My oath has been fulfilled," Lusion debated.

Standing up, Duraturo angrily slammed his fist against his rock chair. "Traitor!" he yelled, pointing a webbed finger at Lusion.

Fiona stood up and placed a hand against Duraturo's chest. "Please, Duraturo, calm yourself," she said, glancing over to Lusion. "You have done my family a great service Lusion. We will forever be in your debt. I ask of you, is there nothing you can do for my people?"

Lusion remained silent.

"What if my men and I infiltrated the city first?" I asked.

The group turned to me as if just remembering I was there. "What good will that do?" Lusion muttered.

"My father has underwater weaponry locked away in his palace. These automatic weapons can only be used by Earth dwellers," Fiona explained.

Lusion gnawed on his thumb deep in thought.

"Once my men have the weapons, we could signal to you, commander. The Nordics wouldn't know what hit them," I tried to reason with him.

"Who would lead you to these weapons?" he asked.

"I will," Fiona said.

"No, you're too valuable," Duraturo objected.

Fiona was about to object, but Ysolda placed a hand on her shoulder, speaking up, "I'll do it."

Silence followed. "You're sure of these weapons' location?" Lusion asked.

Ysolda gave him a confident nod.

"So it's a deal?" I asked him.

I could see him mulling it over in his head. "We have a deal," he finally muttered.

"Great!"

"On one condition," he added, interrupting our celebration. "The weapons must be recovered and turned over to my men at the end of the battle."

"That is fine," Fiona spoke up.

We all shook hands, clearly glad to have an ally. "It's good to have you on our side again," Duaturo told Lusion as the two men embraced with a pat on the back.

Lusion laughed. "We never left your side, you old fish," he joked. The two cracked up and began trading stories with one another, catching up on old times.

Fiona joined my side by the entrance of the den. "Thank you," she whispered, leaning up against the wall of the cave. She gave me a pat on the shoulder with a soft smile across her face.

I shrugged. "It's not a big deal. You would do the same for me."

She stared at me a second. "How can you be so sure?"

"I know you're a person who keeps their word."

She nodded. "You have my word. When this is over, I will do everything in my power to save your daughter."

"Thank you," I whispered.

She nodded. "Follow me. I'll take you back to the others."

CHAPTER 10

After Lusion's agreement to support Fiona in the war, three weeks of preparation followed. The night before the invasion, my group sat around a map model Ysolda had drawn in the sand. "Are there any questions?" she asked as we wrapped up the meeting.

"I've got one," I muttered. I grabbed a stick and pointed toward two towers protecting the main entrance of her father's palace. "What kind of resistance is expected from these towers?"

She shrugged. "We have no way of knowing. The Nordics have completely different tactics than we do. However, archers and boulders are expected to be used as artillery on our approach," she explained.

I nodded my thanks to her. Grant raised his hand. She nodded toward him. "Once we locate the underwater weaponry, what signal are we to use to indicate for the assault to commence?"

"You all will be supplied with a red flare. Firing one off from the watch tower in the middle of the palace will indicate for Lusion's army to attack."

"Any other questions?" she asked, glancing from Grant to Smith to Ryan, and then to me.

The four of us shook our heads, ending the meeting. "Lance, Fiona wishes to speak to you before we leave," Ysolda called to me as we got up preparing to leave.

I gave her a thumbs-up, turned around, and followed the others while Ryan stayed behind, I guess, to flirt for a bit. Fiona turned out to be waiting for us at our den. "Greetings," she called as Grant Smith and I entered.

"What's up?" we called back.

"Where's Ryan?"

"Making out with your sister somewhere," Grant answered.

We all laughed. She rolled her eyes but couldn't stop a smirk from appearing on her face. "This will be the last time that I get to see you all before the battle. I'd like to thank you for your bravery in taking this mission. I promise your effort will not be forgotten. As a token of our appreciation, I've had our hunters prepare a feast for you. Thanks again, boys."

We cheered as a few of her servants came in with a variety of meats and fruits. She came by and shook each of our hands individually. "I'll see you when all this is done and over with," she said.

I nodded my agreement, wishing her luck, before joining Grant and Smith at the stone table and feasting on the meal the Shellians had prepared for us.

It was still dark the next morning when I was shaken awake by Duraturo and his men. "We leave in twenty, Earth dweller."

"Roger," I muttered, wiping the sleep from my eyes.

After shaking awake the others, it was to no surprise that Ryan was absent. I followed the long rocky winding tunnels down to his usual hangout spot to find him and

Ysolda making out. "You two lovebirds even get any sleep?" I called to them.

They glanced at each other and then laughed. "Didn't think so," I muttered.

We left the base right on time and took the four-day hike to Lord Olaf's city pretty much unchallenged. We would run into the occasional scout or patrol but always made it by undetected.

"Is Lusion's army in place?" I whispered to Duraturo, lying flat against the sandy ocean floor and peering down at the city below.

"Yes, we will wait for your signal," he muttered.

I nodded and gulped. I glanced back at my men and Ysolda, motioning for them to come up to my position. "Good luck," Duraturo whispered as we passed.

I glanced back at him. He smiled; it was more of a grimace than anything. That did nothing but tighten the nervous feeling in my gut. I'd been with the Shellians for a month, and he had never smiled once, which could mean only one thing: We were walking straight into a fight we would never forget.

CHAPTER II

Our position was four hundred meters from the nearest structure as we crawled across the open field of weeds masking our approach.

"Fuck me, we're never going to make it there," Smith grunted.

I lifted my belly slightly off the ocean floor, peering through the cover of seaweed at the Shellian city. "Halfway there, man. Come on, we can't stop."

He gritted his teeth and began pulling himself along again. I followed suit. Each time I'd reach out to pull forward, my fingers would sink deep into the sandy ground. It was two grueling hours before we finally reached cover behind a Shellian's home.

"Lead the way," I grunted to Ysolda.

She obediently came up to the front and gave Ryan a kiss while passing by.

"Be careful," he told her.

She smiled. "Yes, mother."

Drawing her bow, she took point, arrow at the ready as we crept from building to building along the edge of the city. Every so often, the Nordic Shellian voices of passing patrols would force us to press up against the mud walls of huts and hold our breath until they passed. After a time, Ysolda held up her hand, signaling a halt, and peeked around the corner.

"Almost there, Lance."

"Where is it?" I asked.

"Right across the street," she answered.

"Is there any cover there?"

She shook her head. "We're going to have to sprint across."

"Let's do it, then."

She held up her webbed hand, counting down from five to one with her fingers.

"Go, go, go!" I whispered urgently as the count ended.

We took off in a dead sprint from the corner of a mud hut toward the staircase leading up to the palace. The panicked cries of civilian Shellians merged into a single sound as we barreled by. The hiss of an arrow flying by our heads, however, was unmistakable.

"Guard shack, Ysolda!"

Her stare followed my finger to the lone guard out front of a barracks. With a quick snap of her wrist, her arrow went flying and hit its mark. The guard crumpled to the ground. He was probably dead before he even knew he'd been shot.

Arrows began spiraling at us from all angles as a deep horn sounded out around the city, warning the Nordics of our presence. "Hurry up the stairs!" Ysolda cried, taking a knee at the staircase and firing back.

We pulled out our knives, charging up to the main door. As we burst in, we were greeted by a hail of arrows. Grant screamed out in pain. We dived behind cover, arrows ricocheting off the floor around us.

"Stay down, Grant!" I called.

He hunkered down behind the fallen stone statue of Lord Olaf in the middle of the entrance. A large arrow protruded from his leg. Blood spewed out and floated in the water around us. The Shellians continued to pepper the fallen statue with arrows.

Grant gritted his teeth, peering over at the wall behind which the Shellians were taking cover. "Leave me. I got these fools!" he cried over to us.

"Smith, stay here and cover his back. Ryan and Ysolda with me," I shouted.

The three of us took off down a long narrow hallway and ran straight into two more guards. Ysolda grabbed her knife and stuck it into the throat of one of them. I wasn't so lucky. As I swiped for the other one's neck, he leaned back, swiping at me. I could feel the searing pain of the knife burying itself in my skin and sliding along my abdomen. Ryan came up behind the guard and drove his machete deep into his back. He fell to the ground, twitching as he succumbed to his wounds.

"Jesus," I grunted, leaning over and applying pressure to the deep slash across my stomach.

"You will not make it far with that cut," Ysolda whispered, taking a quick look at it.

"I'm fine. Let's go," I grunted, forcing myself upright.

Obediently, the two took off running, with me trailing behind. We veered off to the left and burst into a room. Under a rug was a hidden staircase that we followed down to a sealed room.

Ysolda placed her hand against the wall and closed her eyes. "Alipal Kiomotia," she whispered to herself.

Green sparks shot from her hand, racing across the wall

to form the image of the dragon-eel-looking creature her family could turn into. She placed her hand on the image and turned the handle that appeared. There was a rough crack, and a secret door opened, revealing a bare room with nothing but a locked chest in the middle of the floor.

"Bingo," Ryan said, running over to it.

"Move aside, please," Ysolda told him and clenched the lock in a fist.

She squeezed it, whispering a spell to herself, and the lock fell to the ground in pieces. The two of them dug into the chest, taking out the weapons and ammunition. Ryan came over, handing me one of the rifles. I took it in my hands and slung another over my shoulder.

"Meet me at the main entrance," I called to them. I hobbled up the stairs and then down the long, narrow hallway past the two dead guards.

"Grant!" I yelled, smashing through the side door to take cover behind a pillar.

He glanced over at me, relief washing over his face. "Smith's gone!" he yelled, flinching as an arrow smacked the floor beside him.

I glanced across to the other pillar. Smith was lying off to the side of it with an arrow through his chest.

"We need to get to that tower before we're up against the entire city," I called over to him. Cocking one of the rifles, I slid it across the floor to him and unholstered mine. "Ready?"

He gave me a nod. We both peeked around our cover, unloading a fully automatic clip at the staircase in front of us where the Nordics were firing from. We didn't hit anything, but we certainly intimidated them. Panicked yells erupted in front of us. They had probably never seen this kind of fire power before. "Aimed shots," I called out to Grant, slid another mag of ammunition to him, and loaded my own weapon.

He perched the weapon's barrel on the leg of the stone statue and peered through the sight. A Shellian popped his head up over the wall of the staircase. Grant fired. It was the last thing that Shellian would ever do.

I peeked around the stone pillar, searching for another target. One shellian popped up, and Grant shot; but he wasn't fast enough. The Shellian's arrow propelled through the water like a rocket and hit my left shoulder. The force of the blow knocked me to the ground.

"Oh, come on, Grant," I yelled over to him, struggling back behind the pillar and grimaced as I snapped the tail of the arrow off.

"Sorry, that was a fast bugger," he grunted, keeping the sights of his weapon pointed on the staircase.

I reloaded my weapon just in time. My attention shifted as the side door, where Smith's dead body lay, opened. "Three on the left," I shouted to Grant, and nimbly dodged an arrow.

He unloaded a clip into them, killing two. The other lay on the ground, groaning in pain. The Shellian glanced at Grant, who was out of ammo. Yelling in anger, the Shellian reached for a knife on his belt, gritting his teeth in pain. "Uh-oh … Help!" Grant called to me.

I peeked around the pillar, killed the Shellian, and then tossed Grant another mag. The door behind me opened, revealing Ryan and Ysolda. Ryan spotted his brother slumped against the ground and cried out for him.

"Smith, Smith! No … Please, no! Is he still breathing?"

I shook my head, trying to hold him back with my good arm. "He's dead, Ryan. We've got to go."

He pushed me aside.

"No, Ryan!" Ysolda yelled.

It was too late. Ryan took off across the entrance, spraying wildly at the staircase. A hail of arrows was shot at him, one finding its home right in his stomach. "Smith!" he cried out, blood pouring from his mouth as he collapsed to the ground, just short of the statue Grant was taking cover behind.

Grant reached out, pulled Ryan behind cover, snapped the arrow in his own leg, and fired a few potshots at the Shellians above. The door opened, and a wave of them came in to reinforce their position.

"I need to save Ryan!" Ysolda screamed, hiding behind the pillar in front of mine.

"No! If you die, we all die!" I called to her.

The volley of arrows strengthened as the Shellians began to find their range on us.

"God damn it, Lance. We need to get out of here," Grant called.

"There is another way to the tower," Ysolda shouted to me.

"Let's go, then," I answered. And then, "Get your ass over here, Grant."

I began peppering the walls with fire as Grant threw Ryan onto his back and limped across the entrance. Clutching my own stomach, I followed Ysolda through another side door and headed up the staircase into an open field. The tower was sitting there.

Finishing a quick reload, I began to spray at the doors of a building off to our left, covering Grant and Ysolda as they carried Ryan's limp body. Once we were inside, I closed the steel door of the tower and locked it. "Send the signal," Grant urged.

As Ryan struggled for breath, I grabbed my red flare and pulled myself ahead of them up the staircase. Reaching the top, I could see the entire city below scrambling around, not sure what was happening. I unwrapped the flare, aimed it out the side, and then twisted the bottom. It flew into the air, illuminating the whole countryside before exploding in a blinding red light.

War screams erupted from below as the mountainside filled with soldiers charging down toward the city. I slumped to the ground, struggling for breath as I clutched my side in pain. Grant and Ysolda made it to the top before collapsing on the floor in exhaustion.

"We ... we, we did ... it," Ryan managed to say, his body shaking uncontrollably as he gasped for breath.

Ysolda grabbed his hand. Tears were pouring down her face as she nodded and placed a kiss on his forehead. Grant grabbed his other hand. "We couldn't have done it without you, kiddo."

Ryan smiled, trying to say something. I watched his eyes glaze over, his hand went limp, and then, just like that, it was over. He let out a final breath, his head nodding off the side of Ysolda's lap.

She began to sob uncontrollably. "No, please no. Come back, Ryan," she kept whispering.

"He's gone, Ysolda. I'm sorry," I told her.

She shook her head. "I won't let him die, not for my war," she muttered, still sobbing. I tried to hold her, but she pushed me away.

Then I watched in shock as her whole body began to glow. She whispered a spell to herself. The water around us was swirling faster and faster. She leaned down and kissed him. A thunderous boom erupted from above, followed by a white beam of light smashing into her. She lifted her head, screamed in agony, and placed a hand on his chest.

The white light coursed through her body. Ryan began to stir as if in a deep sleep, the redness in his face returning. He opened his eyes. The sea around us became still. The white light evaporated, and he let out a surprised breath of air.

He sat up. "Ysolda?"

She didn't answer. As if on cue, her body fell over, her eyes wide open, dead as a rock. It was then that I realized what she had done. "She gave her life for yours," I whispered to him.

He picked her up in his lap, staring at her still body. "But why?" he asked in sorrow.

"Time will tell," Grant grunted.

I rested my head against the rusted steel beams of the watchtower and stared down as the battle raged. "Her sacrifice will not be forgotten," I promised Ryan before closing my eyes.

Our part in this war below was finally over. For us though, the war above had just begun.

CHAPTER 12

A rescue party was sent up to the tower that night once the battle had been won. The medics immediately attended to us, bandaging our wounds. I saw Fiona appear from behind the crowd. Her face turned pale as she glanced over at her sister's lifeless body.

"Fiona?"

One of the hunters held her back as tears sprang to her eyes. "She's gone, Your Highness," he said, trying to comfort her.

Regaining her composure a short time later, she placed her hands on her hips, staring out to the horizon. I shooed the medic away, pulled myself up, and went to comfort her. "How was she killed?" Fiona asked as I reached her side.

I shook my head. "She wasn't."

"Huh?" Fiona grunted, a confused expression spreading on her face.

"Smith was killed as we assaulted the main staircase. Ryan ran out to save his brother but was shot in the chest. He was still alive when we brought him up here but succumbed to his wounds. Your sister sacrificed her life for his."

Fiona glanced over at Ysolda's still body, which was hugged close by Ryan. He glanced up to her. Their eyes momentarily met. "I'm sorry," I saw him mouth to her.

"Silly girl," she muttered, ripping her eyes back out to the horizon.

"She loved him, Fiona."

"I know. My father always told us growing up never to fall in love. It would be our demise," she said.

"Your father was a fool."

She glanced at me, taken aback by my bold statement. "You know nothing of my father," Fiona replied, her words laced with anger. "He was an honorable man that led our kind to many victories. All this before you could not have been built without him."

"That may be true, but he lived a miserable life and died a bitter man. What Lara and I had experienced the year before I died on that beach was enough to fill a lifetime. I'm sure it was the same between her and Ryan," I said, nodding toward the pair.

She grunted her agreement. "You may be right, but I will never accept her death over an Earth dweller." She paused, thinking to herself. "I have to bury my sister now and then continue the war against the Nordics. I'm very grateful for what you and your men have done for us. Also tell Ryan I'm saddened by his brother's death. My servants will lead you back to your camp."

"Can Ryan not attend her funeral?" I asked.

She shook her head. "It would not be appropriate for an Earth dweller's presence to be felt during the sacred burial of a royal family member."

I went silent. "You will hold true to your promise?"

She nodded, handing me a shell. "When the time is

right, blow this shell anywhere in the sea. I will come and fulfill my end of the deal," she promised.

I stared at the shell, rotating it around in my hand. It felt surreal that it was over. "So I guess this is good-bye?"

She smiled. "For now, Lance."

With a nod of her head, Duraturo picked up Ysolda and led them down the stairs flanked by guards.

"Follow us," one of the hunters ordered.

Ryan glanced at me, confused. "What's going on?"

"It's fine. We are no longer needed here," I told him.

We got up and hobbled down the steps behind the hunters. There were four stretchers waiting for us. Smith's lifeless body had already been placed on one. "Please lie down. We will take you home," one of the hunters said.

Ryan's eyes filled with tears to the sight of his brother's still body. He lay down on the stretcher next to him, followed by Grant and me. It took them three days to carry us to shore.

They had already informed Lara, who was waiting on the beach with a group of others I had never seen before. "Hey, Babe," she whispered, stroking my hair affectionately. Then she took a knee beside my stretcher and gave me a kiss.

I smiled. "Hey, Babe," I whispered, returning the kiss.

"Smith's dead," I told her.

She nodded. "Don't worry about anything. We will take care of it."

I closed my eyes, feeling the ground below me lifted. Two men picked up the stretcher and headed up the cliff toward camp. Rays of sunlight fought their way through the cluster of treetop leaves as we made our way along the dirt path.

Upon entering the camp, we were greeted by Joshua's excited cries. "Grant, Lance, Ryan, you made it!"

I opened an eye, giving the young boy a smile as he ran over to my stretcher with a paper airplane in his hand. "Look what Lara taught me how to make," he said, holding it up proudly.

He offered it to me, and I accepted it in mock amazement. "Wow, that's cool, buddy. Does it fly?"

He nodded. I handed him the plane, and then, with all his might, he threw the plane into the air. It glided twenty meters or so and landed at the foot of a man. I had to squint through the sunlight to make out the figure before laughing to myself.

The hillbilly brothers Jack, Luey, and Steve from Joshua's village stood there. Steve picked up the paper airplane and with a juvenile smile across his face sent it flying back toward Joshua. "Hello, dear fiend killer," he called over to me.

Lara glanced at me, confused. "You know these men?" she asked.

"Grant and I met them in Joshua's village a few days after the massacre," I whispered.

"Aww, great!" I heard Grant mutter as he spotted the brothers. The three of us shared a laugh before the brothers reached our side.

"So you're part of the resistance now?" I asked.

They answered enthusiastically. "Miss Lara Marini here says we be resistance fighters," Steve said.

I laughed, glancing over at Lara, who had a meek smile on her face. "Just call me Lara," she insisted.

Steve bowed his respect to her, his eyes coming to a rest on me. "You should rest up, dear brave fiend killer. I and my brothers will take care of things around here," he said, nodding toward Smith's still body.

I gave him a thankful nod and closed my eyes as Lara placed a kiss on my cheek, a mock smile on her face. "Sleep well, brave fiend killer."

CHAPTER 13

"**L**ance? … Lance! Wake up, Babe."

All I could muster was a rough groan. I opened an eye and was greeted by Lara's beautiful smile.

"What time is it?" I grunted.

"Still early. Everyone is asleep," she replied, handing me an apple.

I accepted it with a grateful nod. She helped me sit up as I winced in pain, staring down at my battle-worn feet. My body ached terribly, but I masked my pain with a smile as Lara took a seat beside me and ate her own apple in silence.

"Have Smith's funeral arrangements been taken care of?" I asked.

She nodded. "Steve and his brothers dug the grave last night. Once the burial is finished, we will meet back here for the reception. Christopher went out at dawn to find a buck for the feast."

"You're the best, Babe," I whispered, and placed a kiss on her cheek. With a sigh, I finished my apple and tossed the core out the door for the birds. "We never should have gone down there," I muttered.

Lara shook her head in disagreement. "It was a calculated

risk that we had to take, Lance. With the Shellians on our side, Rashellia is within our grasp."

"Was it worth Smith's life though?" I questioned.

She went silent before saying, "Many more will die before this is over."

I let out an irritated sigh. She didn't understand that people were dying for our cause. In a way I felt like we were misleading them. They counted on us for survival when in truth we couldn't even take care of ourselves.

"How are the recruitment numbers?" I asked halfheartedly

"Nine. We have another problem though," she began.

"What's that?"

"Some of Goss's men have set up camp here as well," she told me.

"How many?"

"Five or six. It's hard to tell. Some come, and then others leave; it's a constant rotation."

"Don't worry about them. I'll take care of it," I said.

She was about to rebut, but Joshua began to stir behind us, cutting the conversation short. "Morning, buddy," I called over to the little boy. He yawned, sitting up in his bed. He glanced over at me with a sleepy smile, wiping the crud out of his eyes.

Lara got up and retrieved an apple from a bucket in the corner of the hut for his breakfast. As the camp began to spring back to life, I checked over my weapons and gear, making sure no damage had occurred in my absence. Lara helped me wipe down the Timberwolf with gun oil. Shortly afterward, Grant poked his head in, greeting us with a nod.

"Are we ready for Smith's funeral?" he asked.

Lara and I nodded. She held Joshua's hand as we exited

the hut out into the bright mid-September morning, and then they walked on, following a path toward the shoreline where I assumed Smith's funeral would be held.

"Where's Ryan?" I asked Grant.

Grant gave a nod toward the supply hut where Smith's body was being held. "Ryan's saying his good-byes."

Five or six minutes later, Ryan emerged, accompanied by Steve, Jack, and Luey. The six of us grabbed hold of the stretcher holding Smith's body and began our journey down the long, twist-riddled path to the shoreline. As we broke the tree line to the beach, we were welcomed with a dull roar of claps by the reception of those who had gathered to pay their respects. We set the stretcher down beside the grave, which had been dug beneath a tall spruce.

A man whom I had not yet met stepped out of the crowd and walked to the grave, where he began the ceremony. I stared up as slivers of light danced their way through the looming branches of the spruce. In a way, I knew that Smith was with his son now, and that thought alone was enough to bring a smile to my face. Once the funeral was done, the soldiers began to scatter, heading back to camp in their individual groups. Grant decided to stay at the beach and talk with Ryan, which I figured was for the best. He had gone through a similar experience when he lost Ellie during a patrol in the Harush Forest.

There was a somber mood back at camp. No one had really known Smith, but out of respect for his brother, no one was blatantly careless about the loss of a resistance fighter. Lara took the opportunity to introduce me to some of the troops.

The first was a strong young kid of about twenty-three, who was off to the side of the camp, skinning a deer for the reception. He stopped what he was doing as we approached, greeting us with a wave. Lara introduced us: "Lance, I'd like you to meet Christopher."

I offered my hand to him. With a strong grasp, he gave it a shake out of respect.

"Where are you from, man?" I asked.

"North Harush," he replied.

"You were NWO?"

He shook his head. "They kept trying to get me to join, but I refused. I've lived off these lands with my two sisters ever since the war started."

I folded my arms across my chest, trying to act like a leader as I gave him a thankful nod for joining us. "It's good to have you on board. Your sisters are staying here as well?"

He tilted his head toward the center of the camp. There was a little girl of about nine or ten playing with Joshua. The two of them had sticks, and they were slapping them together as they had an imaginary sword fight with each another. The three of us chuckled, watching them play for a moment.

"I'm glad you guys made it. Joshua has been in desperate need of a friend. Lara and I can only do so much for the poor kid."

Christopher grunted his agreement. "Same with Jessica. Ever since she lost her sister, she's changed. Being a grown man, there's only so much I can do to try to relate to her."

I gave him an apologetic look, cluing in to the fact that the other sister had been killed. "I'm sorry for your loss."

He thanked me but brushed away my condolences. "Really, the dead ones are the lucky ones. They don't need to deal with this war anymore."

I nodded my agreement.

"What's the deal with Joshua?" he asked.

"His mother was killed in a fiend raid on his village."

We watched the kids play for a few more minutes in silence. "Well, I suppose Lara and I should get going. I don't want to keep you from your work," I said, glancing at the half-skinned deer.

"All right, thank you. It was nice meeting you," he replied, his attention shifting back to the deer.

Lara and I walked together along the perimeter of the camp, watching the life in its midst. Some people busily worked on their shelters while others were playing cards or hanging their wet clothes out to dry. Now and then, Lara would point to key people who had joined, giving me the lowdown on everyone.

"Those are the NWOs?" I asked, spotting a hut off to the edge of the camp with an armed guard sitting outside on a bench and tending to a smoldering fire.

She nodded. "Aren't exactly the cheery kind," she grunted under her breath. "Hey, wait. No, Lance," she objected, trying to pull me back as I broke off our course and headed over to the hut.

I ignored her warning and strutted over toward the guard. He seemed a little taken aback that I was willing to talk with them. He put on a fake smile and greeted us as we stopped on the other side of the fire. "Afternoon, sir."

I nodded, placing my own fake smile on. "Afternoon. Who is your highest-ranking member here?" I asked.

"Uh, Sergeant Talbot," he muttered.

"I'd like to speak with him."

"Certainly, sir, just give me a second to get him."

"That won't be necessary," I replied, taking the soldier by surprise as I pushed past him through the door. I was greeted by the sight of five soldiers, lying half-dressed on their make shift beds. They all stared at me in shock as Lara and the soldier pushed their way in behind me.

"I'm looking for Sergeant Talbot," I said as the soldier behind me began to sputter his apologies for letting me barge in.

An older man in his thirties held up his hand to the sputtering soldier, got off his bed, and met me in the middle of the hut. "You must be Lance," he muttered with a halfhearted smile. We shook hands, staring each other down.

"You must be Talbot," I grunted, with an unimpressed smirk.

He returned the smirk, giving a nod down to my holstered pistol. "You could get shot barging into someone's place uninvited with a loaded weapon."

I chuckled to myself, not fazed at all by his threat. "You have six soldiers here with weapons, and you're worried about one battered-up, pistol-carrying sniper taking out your men?" I asked.

Without warning I made a move toward my pistol. The NWO fighters instinctively reached for their weapons. I laughed, holding up my hands. "Just messing around, boys. Jeez, you guys are on a short leash," I teased them.

Sergeant Talbot gave me an unamused look, taking a sip from his coffee. "Is there something I can help you with?"

I shook my head. "Just a friendly-neighbor call. That's all."

"Then get out," he grunted.

I laughed. "As you wish. By the way, there will be a feast tonight in honor of one of our fallen. We're all on the same team here. If you boys would like to come out and get some grub, you're more than welcome," I said.

Talbot smirked as I turned to leave the hut. "Can't help but feel like that poor kid would still have his brother, if he wasn't dragged into a pointless excursion with the Shellians," he teased.

Anger at his bold statement coursed through my veins. I could feel my face turning red, and it took everything I had to restrain myself from killing him. I glanced back with rage in my eyes. "You sit here and enjoy that coffee, you piece of shit. I'll let you boys know when the war's over."

The clink and clank of weapons being picked up instantly followed my statement. Sergeant Talbot held up his hands to the soldiers, letting me go. "You have yourself a good night, Lance."

Lara and I took our leave and strolled about thirty or forty feet before Lara grabbed my arm, yanking me to a stop. "Are you crazy, Lance?" she hissed in anger.

"We can't let them walk over us like that. This is our camp, not theirs," I said.

She shook her head in disbelief. "Our fate lies in their hands, Lance. If we break allegiance with them, the NWO will crush us."

All I could muster was an annoyed sigh. I knew she was right. As I stared at the camp fires coming to life in the gathering dusk, I knew we couldn't worry about the NWO. We had a much larger threat looming in the distance, a common enemy that we and the fiends both shared. A cold breeze cut through my windbreaker, sending me the chilling reminder that winter was coming.

CHAPTER 14

One month later

A savage wind tore through the bare trees, celebrating the first of November, and what leaves still clung on to the branches were swept away, leaving us to embrace the elements. We had made a return trip to Joshua's old village a few weeks earlier to pick up what clothes and supplies we could to survive the winter, but it wasn't enough. Our numbers had grown to thirty-five fighters and a handful of women and children, who all looked to us for protection. After three days of hiding in our shelters and living off of potatoes and water, we had to make another supply run.

Although our alliance was shaky, the NWO agreed to come with us as their own individual group, while I handpicked Grant, Steve, and Christopher to join me. Sergeant Talbot knew of a village about twenty kilometers away that the New World Order frequently went to for supplies.

"You guys be safe out there," Lara told me as we got ready to leave, assault rifles slung over our empty backpacks.

"Always am," I joked, and gave her a kiss.

Joshua came up to me to say his goodbye just as I glanced over at Christopher and Jessica hugging each other farewell. "You take care of her, all right?" I told Joshua.

He glanced from Jessica to me, nodded with a huge smile, and gave me the thumbs-up. "I won't let any bad fiends in this camp," he promised.

I laughed, returning the thumbs-up, and then we set off, following Sergeant Talbot and his men. It took over half a day to reach the outskirts of the village. My heart sank at first glance, as the village appeared to be abandoned, but after five minutes or so of surveillance, we could see signs of life around the village as a mother came onto the deck of her hut to hang out clothes.

"All right, boys, only take what we need. Be polite. We are here to ask for support, not to pillage," I reminded everyone. My guys all agreed. I glanced at Talbot, who grunted his agreement. Then we got up from our concealment and headed toward the village.

My men and I started from the front of the village, and the NWOs began from the back. The old, worn steps of the first hut let out eerie creaks as I walked up to the entrance. I tapped on the door, slinging my rifle down off my shoulder to appear as nonthreatening as possible. There was no answer. I glanced back at Grant questioningly. All he could offer was a shrug. As I turned to leave, I heard a rustle from inside.

"Hello?" I called out.

Nothing happened. I let out a frustrated sigh, heading back down the steps.

"Lance," Grant called, pointing behind me.

I turned to see the door slightly cracking open. An elderly man was there, with a small child hugging his leg in fear.

"Hello there, sir. My name is Lance Burns. My men and I were wondering if you had any food or supplies you could spare for the resistance this winter."

"You're the NWO?" he asked.

I shook my head. "The Revolutionary Force."

He mouthed the name to himself before chuckling. "You're all the same. Come here and pillage us innocent villagers. You guys are nothing more than bandits."

I gave him a frustrated sigh but a respectful nod. "Thank you for your time, sir."

Glancing down the path to the NWO, I could see that they weren't having much better luck.

"Glad we walked twenty kilometers for this," Grant muttered in frustration.

I laughed, slapping his back on the way to the next house. "We'll get something. Don't you worry."

A single mother was the next to answer. I began to introduce myself when I heard banging coming from down the street. I peeked around the door to see Sergeant Talbot and his men breaking into a hut. "Hey!" I shouted at them.

They ignored my calls, forcing me to run over to them. "What the hell are you guys doing?" I asked Talbot.

"Back up, Lance. We tried it your way; now we're doing it our way."

I could hear the panicked cries of children from inside as Talbot's men continued to bash at the door with the butts of their weapons. "Back up, boys," he yelled, drawing his weapon and taking aim at the door.

"Stop!" I ordered. He didn't listen firing a burst into the door which was followed by a cry of agony. Without thinking, I drew my pistol, took aim, and fired. It was a direct hit into the back of Talbot's skull. He fell to the ground, twitching and gurgling uncontrollably.

Time seemed to have frozen as both sides drew their weapons. My side was faster; we annihilated the NWO with only a few but accurate shots. The kid that had been guarding Talbot's hut the first day I met him was the only one to survive. He lay on the porch, screaming in pain as he clutched his leg. "Grant, patch him up," I ordered, holstering the pistol.

My hand would not stop shaking. I knew I had done the right thing, but ultimately, saving the innocents had sealed our fate. Timidly, I opened what remained of the door. A mother was on all fours crying; her son had been hit in the shoulder.

"Look, what you've done, you savage!" she screamed in rage, and spit in my direction as I held my hands up peacefully.

"It wasn't my men, ma'am. Look, we killed them. They won't be bothering you anymore."

She glanced around me to the foot of the door, where she saw the dead NWO soldiers. I pulled out my medical kit.

"Hey there, buddy. What's your name?" I asked the kid. He cringed in pain as I poured water on the wound and began bandaging it up with a field dressing.

"Tyler."

"You're going to be just fine, Tyler," I comforted him, snapping on a safety pin to keep the field dressing from coming off. I turned to his mother.

"Thank you," she whispered apologetically.

"I would have reacted the same way had it been my daughter," I told her comfortingly. I paused, glancing back at her son. "He will need to come back to our base with us in order to remove the bullet from his shoulder."

She nodded. "I'm coming as well."

"I know this is a terrible time to ask, but would you have any food or supplies you could donate to the resistance?"

She paused, glancing up at me in thought. "May we stay with you?" she asked.

I nodded. "All are welcome in our camp."

She gave me a thankful smile. "Take what you can carry, then."

I felt myself jump for joy inside, having hit a gold mine. "Thank you, ma'am."

I helped Tyler up and led his mother and him to the door, where Steve greeted them and led them away.

"How's he doing?" I asked Grant, who was finishing up what he could do for the wounded NWO soldier.

"We need to get him out of here as fast as we can, or he's going to bleed out," Grant said.

The soldier's eyes filled with fear. "Please, Lance, I beg you. I'll do anything."

I gave him a reassuring smile, kneeling down beside him and patting his shoulder. "Don't worry, buddy. You'll be fine. Grant, did you bring your ranger blanket?"

He nodded and pulled it out of his backpack. I took two logs and rolled the blanket around them, forming a stretcher. Grant and I lay the soldier on it and called over Christopher and Steve. "Take him back to camp as fast as you can," I ordered. Then I unloaded the dead soldiers' weapons, put the ammo, jackets, gloves, and tuques into their backpacks, and strapped their weapons to the sides of the packs.

"What about the woman and her kid?" Steve asked.

"They can come with us," I ordered. "Go now."

Obediently, the two picked up the stretcher and began a light trot down the path toward camp. I let out a sigh of relief.

People were beginning to appear on their decks to stare at us. "Let's go get the stuff in there," I whispered to Grant, nodding toward the door. He followed me in. There was a spare room filled with canned food, potatoes, and other nonperishable items. I loaded them into my backpack while Grant stocked up his with other supplies such as blankets and warm clothing for the winter. The woman appeared at the door with Tyler, watching us curiously. "Is there anything I can do?" she asked.

I nodded. "Grab one of those dead soldier's backpacks and stuff it with as much food as you can carry." She did so, and less than ten minutes later, we were ready to go. As we left, the whole village began to clap. I smiled to myself, knowing we had done a good thing. Goss, however, would not see it that way.

We did not arrive back at camp until maybe one or two in the morning. Lara was outside, pacing back and forth. Relief instantly washed over her tense face at the sight of us. "I heard what happened. Are you all right?" she asked.

Grant and I nodded. "The kid is shot in his shoulder."

She glanced over at Tyler and his mother as if just noticing their presence. "Please follow me," she said with a light smile.

We all went to the medical hut, sat the boy down, and unbandaged the wound to inspect it. I glanced over at a cot in the corner where Christopher was guarding the NWO soldier.

"Good to see you made it," I told the soldier, approaching his cot.

He gave me a halfhearted smile. "Thank you for all you've done."

"No problem. You're in good hands now," I said. I gave Christopher a thankful pat on the back. "I'll stay and keep watch on him for a bit. Go get some rest."

"Thanks, man. Have a good night," he muttered. He grabbed his weapon and took his leave out the back door.

The NWO soldier glanced over at Tyler with a guilty look. "Will he be all right?"

I nodded. "Just a clean shot through his shoulder."

He gave a thankful nod. His lower lip was trembling as he let out a defeated sigh, staring at the rafters. "I didn't want anyone to get hurt. They were the ones who tried to break in, and they never listened to me. I didn't even want to join the stupid resistance, but what choice did I have? It was them or the fiends."

"I know. It's fine. We all make mistakes. Trust me when I tell you I'm the guiltiest one of that here," I told him.

He laughed, extending his hand to me. "I'm Pat."

"Good to meet you, Pat. I'm Lance," I said, giving his hand a firm shake.

"So what now?" he asked.

I shrugged. "Goss is not going to be happy about this. When are your replacements expected?"

"We were to stay here until spring," he told me.

I let out a sigh of relief. With Goss in the black about what had happened, I would have some time to figure out a plan.

"Would Talbot send him reports?" I asked.

He nodded. "Weekly."

"Good, you're my new messenger," I informed him.

He smiled. "Happy to be of service."

It took close to three weeks for Pat to recover from his wounds. When he did, I wrote a note to Goss, informing him that the others had been killed in a firefight with the fiends. It was a very likely story. Whether Goss would buy it or not was a different one altogether.

"You nervous?" I asked Pat.

He nodded.

"Good. Just don't let them see that. If they find out, it will be both our heads."

"I won't," he promised.

With a pat on the back from me, he left the camp in the direction of the NWO headquarters. I felt a set of arms wrap around my waist and glanced back to see Lara staring at Pat as he left.

"Do you think this will work?" she whispered.

"What other choice do we have?"

She remained silent as her hand crept down along my waist. Her fingers were intertwining with mine. I gave her a questioning look. She giggled, leading me into our hut.

"Where's Joshua?" I asked, staring at the empty bed space.

"He's playing with Jessica," she assured me. I began to protest, but she simply placed a finger on my lips, whispering, "Shh."

Taking off her shirt, she guided my hand up to her bare chest. I closed my eyes, succumbing to her will. I gave her one last kiss before lying down in our bed.

"Was that to my man's perfection?" she panted once we had finished.

I laughed, giving her an affectionate nod. We cuddled

for a little while, not saying anything. There was no need to; we knew we loved each other. I'd tickle her side, she'd giggle, giving me a playful slap, and we would exchange a few affectionate stares or kisses.

It felt like forever since we had last had time to ourselves. Between Joshua, the war, and recruiting, there was no time for anything else. I rested my head in her arms as she purred affectionately, feeling comfort for the first time in a long time.

The illusion of happiness didn't last long though. Soon afterward, I awoke to a shrill scream outside. Lara and I threw on our clothes and raced outside to the source of the commotion.

"What's going on here?" I yelled, pushing my way through the crowd. I gulped; a sinking feeling hit my stomach. What I saw next was enough to make any man tremble.

Pat, the NWO soldier I had sent to Goss with a message, had returned with Goss's response. His head was fixed on top of a stick pegged into the ground, with the word *traitor* carved into a wooden sign at the bottom.

"Get everyone out of here," I ordered, turning to Lara.

She remained silent, staring at the sign with fear in her eyes. When I gave her a rough shake her attention shifted to me as if she were just realizing where she was.

"Get them out of here," I repeated.

"Uh ... Yes ... you're right," she finally said, turning around and helping some soldiers break the crowd up.

I ripped the sign out of the ground and cringed, staring at Pat's head in my hand. Grant grabbed a shovel, and we buried him a few minutes away from camp.

"How the hell did they set that up without anyone

noticing?" was the only question I could ask once we had gotten back to camp.

Grant shrugged. "Luck, I guess."

With a sigh, I shook my head in disappointment. "Double all present patrols around the area. The fiends aren't our only enemies now."

CHAPTER 15

Winter hit us with no mercy a month later. Joshua lay huddled between Lara and me as the wind raged outside. It was the third snowstorm in less than two weeks.

"If this keeps up, we won't make it to January," Lara whispered, stroking the sleeping child's head.

"What do you want me to do?" I returned, in frustration.

She shook her head. "I'm just saying, Babe."

"I know," I replied, staring unhappily at our hut's flickering fire.

There was a rustle at the door, causing me to glance up. Grant, Christopher, and Ryan came in, shaking the snow off their clothes.

"What's the word?" they asked curiously, gathering around the fire.

"No hunting trip today. We can't risk it," I told them.

I glanced from face to face. Some were bummed by the news, knowing it meant another day of potato soup, but I knew that the general consensus of the group would be one of relief at not having to battle the elements only to come back empty-handed.

"How's water?" I asked Grant.

He gave me a thumbs-up. "We've been boiling snow and rationing it out to the huts. Some people are a little dehydrated, but nothing too serious," he reported.

"What's the plan for food tonight?" I asked, glancing over at Christopher.

"We have some extra deer meat from last night. I'll add a few pieces into the potato soup tonight to tide people over until the storm passes," he said.

I nodded my thanks and asked Ryan, "Lastly, how's our wood supply?"

He shook his head. "Not good. After supper, we are going to have to stop issuing wood; otherwise we won't have enough if this storm continues into tomorrow."

"Nonsense. We have women, children, and the elderly. We can't just cut off heat. They will die," I debated.

"We all will die if we don't," came his rebuttal.

"What if we kept one hut heated all night?" I asked.

He bit his lower lip, staring into space in thought. "I suppose we could do that."

"Good. After supper, round up the ones most in need of a warm shelter and place them in the meal hall. It is the biggest, so it will serve as the best shelter. Any questions?" I asked.

They remained silent. "Good. I'll see you guys tomorrow," I told them with a nod.

They obediently got up and headed out to complete their tasks. Lara smiled and gave me a kiss. "We will make it," she said. I nodded my hopefulness.

An hour later, Grant came in with soup. Lara shook Joshua awake as Grant took a seat beside me. He took the bowls and poured us each our ration.

"A meal fit for a king," Grant joked, trying to lighten up the mood.

I smirked. "Think I was fed better in prison."

Lara giggled, giving me a playful shot to my ribs.

"I'm still hungry," Joshua complained, setting his bowl down.

I stepped in. "You know what, buddy? Today's your lucky day. I'm stuffed. Don't think I can eat another bite." I handed him the rest of my bowl.

"Lance," Lara objected. I held my hand up to her.

Joshua's smile went from ear to ear as he thanked me, digging into what was left of the soup. I glanced over at Lara, who mouthed, "I love you."

"Jeez, did you even breathe?" Grant asked as Joshua slurped up what was left. He shook his head playfully. Lara wiped off his mouth and gave him a kiss on his forehead.

"You're going to go with Grant to the meal hall to sleep tonight. Jessica and the others are there for you to play with," she told him.

"Aw, but I want to stay with you and Lance," he replied.

Lara glanced at me, but I shook my head. "It's going to be too cold, buddy. Maybe tomorrow."

I could see his disappointment, but he didn't argue. After supper, he obediently said his goodbyes before following Grant out the door. I waited a few moments to make sure they weren't returning before offering Lara my wrist. "Drink, Babe. You haven't had any blood for a few days now."

She nodded, gently grasping my arm. Her eyes turned blood red as fangs protruded from her mouth and sank into my arm. After drinking, she wiped the blood from her mouth.

"All better?" she whispered as she ran her hand along my arm, healing the wound.

I nodded, then spotted a few tears trickling from her eyes, which she tried to hide. "What's wrong, Babe?"

She giggled, waving her hand at me. "It's nothing. Just stupid female emotions," she told me.

I laughed, wrapping my arms around her as she lay down in my lap. "It's okay, Babe. You can tell me," I said.

"Every time I see you with Joshua, I can't help but think about Rashellia," she said.

I nodded understandingly. "We will get her back."

The fire flickered, slowly beginning to smolder as what was left of our ration of wood burned away. I watched our shadows dancing around the walls of the hut in silence as Lara purred contently to herself. An hour later, with one last puff of smoke, the fire went out, leaving us in darkness. The hut's temperature instantly plummeted, as what heat was left escaped through the walls.

"I'll transform, Babe," Lara offered.

I nodded my agreement. Moments later, the cracking of her bones could be heard. I felt the fur sprouting all across her body, completing the transformation. Contentedly snuggling into her belly, I was instantly greeted by warmth.

Five or six hours later, I was awakened by a rough shake. "Ungh?" I grunted, making out the dull outline of Grant.

"Trouble at the outpost," he whispered.

"Be right out," I muttered, wiping the crust from my eyes.

Careful not to wake Lara, I slipped on my jacket and boots. I cursed under my breath as I left the comfort of the hut for the icy December air.

"What's going on?" I muttered.

"The outpost is reporting movement by the NWO," he reported.

I followed him up the rocky ledge to our outpost, where Steve and his two brothers were diligently watching their assigned areas.

"What's up, boys?" I greeted them.

Steve put his finger on his mouth, pointing to the other end of the field. I followed it and spotted torches in the tree line at the outer edge of the field.

"Dem be fiends?" he asked.

I shook my head. "Probably an NWO platoon," I whispered back, looking through the sight picture of my Timberwolf to make out the silhouettes of armed men setting up camp. "Grant, go back and fetch me the mortars and a few fighters."

He did so, returning six or seven minutes later with Christopher and a few other men. We patted down the snow and set up two mortar pits. Grant then took off a backpack containing what we had for mortar rounds and laid them on the ground on top of a blanket.

"Only twelve," he told us.

"We'll have to make them count," I answered.

I pulled out a pair of binoculars and used the built-in laser rangefinder. "Six hundred meters," I called back to them, as two teams of three manned the mortars. "Grant, your team fire at six hundred; Christopher, your team fire at seven hundred and each of you drop fifty after each shot; Grant, you walk the mortars left; and Chris, you walk the mortars right. Don't fire until my mark," I ordered.

I took aim through my sniper, adjusted my elevation as I traversed the gun from right to left, and followed the silhouette of a soldier. My breathing slowed, and my finger clasped the trigger. My shot hit its mark, and the soldier dropped dead, like a sack of potatoes.

There were panicked cries from the other side of the field, but it was too late. The sound of mortars filled the air. Trees were mowed down as Grant and Christopher landed square on their targets and began traversing from left to right. The muzzle blast of machine guns began to light up from the enemy positions, forcing me to cower behind the safety of the ledge. A brief pause was all it took for me to regain my sight picture and take out one of the gunners.

"Get that machine gun over here!" I yelled to Steve.

He set up his firing position beside me and began to fire in slow burst, suppressing the enemy as a para flare shot up into the sky and illuminated the battlefield. The cries of fear coming from camp a hundred meters away sent a constant reminder of what was at stake if we failed to repel them.

"Conserve your ammo, Steve," I shouted. "Grant, go get help. We need ammo, radios, and para flares."

He obediently scrambled off toward the camp, sending snow everywhere as he stumbled down the hill. I cursed under my breath as the NWO began to hammer us with a few of their own mortars. "Everyone conserve your ammo," I called across the line as my men began to potshot the forest below, while mortars rained in around us.

Once Grant had returned with ammunition and reinforcements, I peeled back with Christopher, Ryan, and him to make a plan while the others kept the NWO suppressed.

"They're probing us to see our defenses. We need to take a squad down around the forest line and cut off their escape," I yelled, trying to compete with the sounds of the explosions around us.

"We should hold the line!" Ryan yelled back.

I shook my head. "If they make it back to Goss, he will know that he can attack us at will. We need to send him a clear message that his war with us is not worth it," I argued.

"You want us to risk slaughtering the entire platoon?" Christopher asked.

"It's the only way. Otherwise, they will keep doing this until we run out of supplies and ammunition. The mortars did most of the legwork. They will be slow with their wounded. I need myself and four others. Who's with me?"

Grant gave me a nod, and so did Christopher. "I'll stay and control things here," Ryan offered.

I agreed. Because he had just lost his brother, his mind wouldn't be clear for this excursion, anyway. "Once we have secured the location, I will fire a red para flare," I told him, turning to our soldiers fighting on the ridge line. "Jack, Steve, Luey, follow me!" I yelled up to the line of rebels firing down at the forest below.

The three of them came stumbling down the hill and came to a rest at our feet. "We're flanking them. Let's go."

"Er, wait, dear fiend killer," Steve began to protest.

I didn't give him time to finish the sentence; Grant, Christopher, and I took off down toward the tree line. I glanced back, trying to stifle my laughter as the three fellows came racing after us. Following the tree line, we made it to the NWO's position. I moved ahead of the others and peered through a dense cluster of pine trees, spotting a machine gun crew.

I could hear orders being shouted, and it appeared that they were organizing a retreat. I slipped silently back to the others, motioning for them to follow. A hundred meters down, there was a water crossing where two trees had fallen, forming a natural bridge.

The ice was too thin for the enemy camp to cross. The only way they could make their escape was over these trees. We climbed across, setting up the ambush on a small knoll on the other side. It wasn't long afterward that the gunfire of the battle sputtered into silence. I pulled out my grenade and held it up for the others to see. They nodded, plugged their ears with their hands, and crouched behind cover.

The forest in front of us began to spring to life as the sounds of soldiers and rustling of trees filled the air. I pulled the pin on the grenade and kept it firmly in my hand. Ten or so soldiers emerged from the bushes, crossing the fallen trees. I chucked the grenade; the ground trembled as it exploded and sent most of them flying. Then Steve and the others opened fire, spraying fully automatic bursts into the stunned group. None of them survived. We raced down to the bodies of the dead soldiers and collected ammunition, whatever weapons we could carry, and intel.

Following their trails, we found their attack position, where seven soldiers lay dead, face down in the snow, and four others lay groaning in pain, clearly abandoned. I reached for my pistol but felt Grant's firm grasp clutch my hand. I glanced at him questioningly. He shook his head. "They're not a threat, Lance."

I glanced from him to the wounded soldiers, holstered the pistol, and walked a few more feet out into the open tree line where I shot a red para flare signaling our victory. Cheers erupted from the cliff as our men appeared from behind cover, holding their weapons up triumphantly.

"*Is it over?*" Lara's thoughts came floating into mine.

"*Yes, Babe. We won. Is everyone all right back there?*"

"Yeah, we're fine. The kids are just scared. That's all," she replied.

"Tell everyone not to worry. We just need to grab supplies. There are four wounded here who will need medical attention. Get a fire started in the medical hut," I told her.

"Okay, Babe. Be safe," she told me.

I glanced back at Grant, who was digging through the coat pocket of a dead soldier. "Bingo!" he cried, happily retrieving a pack of smokes from the soldier's jacket.

I laughed, splitting a cigarette with him as we waited for the others to come pick up the supplies we needed.

"Do you think there will be more?" he asked, glancing at the dead soldiers scattered around us.

All I could offer was a shrug. I took a puff of the smoke and handed it back.

"If there is, we will be ready."

CHAPTER 16

After the attack, the NWO left us alone for the rest of the winter, lulling me into a false sense of security. We had lost three soldiers in the assault, and another four had been wounded, but all in all, as weird as it is to say, that night was the best thing that could have happened to us. We were now well stocked with ammunition, clothing, weapons, and food. We had even obtained a ten-man arctic tent, which was great for the kids to play in.

Out of the four soldiers we had found wounded, only two survived. We gave them the choice to stay with us or return back to their camp. To no surprise, they chose to stay with us. Stories of our victory had spread across the region, greatly helping with recruitment as fighting aged men from all over flocked to our camp to join the Revolutionary Force, swelling our numbers up to around a hundred by the time the snow had melt, allowing spring to set in.

Our rapid growth caused a lot of logistical problems, such as food and shelter, forcing us to send out double the supply runs. Fiona also agreed to help out. Her men would deliver us a portion of their daily catch in return for our support against the Nordics every now and then. On an early April morning, however, I was taught the harsh lesson to never become complacent. Peacefully hammering on our hut, Lara and I worked diligently at replacing a rotting side piece when I heard the unfamiliar sound of gunfire break out nearby. In shock I glanced up the hill where our outpost would have been realizing they were under attack.

"Grant! Grab the men!" I shouted over to him as we dropped everything to take cover.

The sounds of mortars began raining in all around us as our base was peppered with indirect fire. I glanced up at the outpost, watched smoke billow from it, and cursed under my breath as I crawled into our hut to retrieve my Timberwolf and TacVest. Civilians scattered into the wood line as practiced.

I jumped onto Lara as she transformed, and we took off into the air and circled. With a glance down at the scene, I took in the sights of the attack before being forced to duck back behind her as tracers ripped through the air. The NWO soldiers scattered, beginning their retreat from the smoldering outpost down across the meadow back toward their base. "*What should we do?*" Lara's voice echoed into my head.

"*There's nothing we can do ... We will do more harm than good trying to chase them,*" I explained back through our telepathic communication, cursing to myself in anger. "*Take us back down,*" I told her with a reassuring pat on the back. She let out her lion-like roar at them and plummeted back down to our camp.

We landed in the middle of the encampment, and I hopped off her and jogged across to Grant and his men, who had six mortars set up and returned fire into the meadow ahead of our outpost. "Cease fire!" I shouted to them, motioning my hand back and forth across my neck.

The order went racing down the line. Grant got up and walked over to me with a confused stare. "We're not going after them, Lance?"

I shook my head. "They can have this one. We have wounded to take care of," I ordered.

He let out an unhappy sigh, placed his hands against his hips, and bit on his bottom lip in disappointment. Giving me one last look, he turned to his men and ordered them to stand down. "We will get them back," I promised, giving him a gentle pat on his shoulder before turning back to Lara, who had transformed back to her human form.

One of the men blew into his whistle in three sharp consecutive blows, signaling the all clear. Our civilians began to return to camp, fire smoldering from some of the huts that had been hit as our dead lay strewn across the ground all around us. I felt sick to my stomach. I knew they needed me to say something, but I just turned on my heels, stormed back to my hut, and tossed my kit into a pile at the back of the cabin.

Lara came in, sat down by my side, and remained silent while I wept unhappily into my arms, comforted by her soft "Shh" as she stroked me.

"It's my fault," I sniffled, wiping away a handful of tears. "I should have seen this coming."

"Don't be silly," Lara scolded me. "You're a twenty-one-year-old commander. Mistakes happen, Lance. We will get them back."

"Tonight," I muttered vengefully.

She glanced down with a nod and gave me a kiss on my neck. "Your command is my will," she whispered, leaving my side momentarily to pour herself and me a glass of water.

"Whom will you take?" she asked, taking a seat and offering me the glass.

I gave her a grateful nod, sipped on it thoughtfully, stared at the ground, and finally shook my head. "No one. I don't want these men paying for my mistakes anymore. I'll finish this myself."

"Lance ..." She paused, giving me an unhappy stare. "There are hundreds of soldiers. You will never make it out alive."

"It only takes one bullet to cut the head off the snake," I explained with full confidence behind my plan.

"Goss?" she whispered.

I nodded while retrieving the Timberwolve's silencer from my backpack, attaching it to the weapon. Before examining the set of four Claymores I had in there. The crack of our hut's door opening forced me to glance up. Grant entered the room, the grim news he carried present on his face. "Seventeen killed, thirteen wounded," he said.

"There's nothing you could have done, man. The lone responsibility rests on my shoulders," I told him, walking over and placing a reassuring hand on his shoulder.

"We should have followed them," he muttered, brushing my hand away and still angered by my decision.

I shook my head and nodded toward my kit. His eyes followed my stare over to it. He took note of the ghillie suit and sniper prepped for tonight. "What will you do?" he asked bitterly.

"Something I should have done long ago," I promised.

A crowd was gathered around my hut that night. Civilians and soldiers all alike gathered around in silence.

I stared at them. All were shocked. Lara stood fully transformed; the crowd had split to form a pathway to her.

No one said a word. It was a somber mood as I nodded to them and began to walk through the crowd of people. Some would reach over and pat me on the shoulder. Others would give a hug, tearing up.

They erupted into cheers as I climbed up onto Lara, waved my good-byes, and began firing celebrating shots on top the air, chanting my name. *"Let's do this, Lara,"* I whispered through my head, and she obediently let out her roar. She sprinted across the camp and then tossed herself into the air, her magnificent wings unfolding as we flew off into the night's cover, skimming along the treetops as the whooshing sound of her flapping wings was the only thing left to keep us company. An hour later, she began to slow as we approached the outskirts of the New World Order's camp, only being another ten or so kilometers away. She landed in an open field, setting me down.

"I will stay here until you return," she whispered into my head.

I shook mine furiously, knowing the chances of me making it out alive were slim to none. *"You go back and take care of Joshua. He will need you. So will the camp. If I don't return, Grant is in charge, and when the day comes that you do have our daughter back in your arms, make sure she knows how much she meant to me,"* I told her. I said my good-byes, unclipped the heart pendant of my family, and gave it to her.

"But Lance ..." she began to protest before I waved her objections away.

"Promise me, Lara."

"*I promise,*" she whispered back, nuzzling her muzzle against me.

I gave it a kiss and her head one last pat. Then she turned, taking off back into the direction we had come from. "I love you," I whispered to myself, watching her fly safely away into the clouds.

I threw my ghillie suit's hood over my head, crouched down into the weeds, took out my map for a quick look, and jotted down a few mental notes on possible routes to the camp, which was fourteen kilometers away, realizing I could follow a winding river all the way.

I folded up the map and jogged into the wood line. It took only a few minutes for me to hit the river that was displayed on the map. I followed it for two or three hours in silence until the sounds of the rebel encampment began to waft their way through the trees as I neared.

Once I had a visual on the camp, I glanced at my watch reading twenty-two hundred. Knowing it was going to be a long night, I hunkered down in a few ferns on the edge of the camp, watching as life played out oblivious to my presence. There was a party raging on in the distance. A lot of soldiers were gathered around a fire, probably celebrating their victory over us this morning.

Taking a breath, I brought up the sight picture of my sniper rifle. I scanned along the party and finally found my target. Goss was sitting next to a fire with a whole bunch of what looked like his higher-ups, and a female was sitting on his lap. "Motherfucker," I whispered to myself as he shared a beer with one of his buddies.

At about two in the morning, the party life began to dissipate as soldiers and civilians returned back to their shacks. I followed Goss through my scope. The girl stood up, held out her hand, and led him into a shack not too far from the bonfire, which had been raging on all night.

I packed up my stuff and slowly crawled into the encampment before taking cover behind a hut where I stood up, peering around the corner to the shack where the woman and Goss had retreated to. Two men stood guard outside. Glancing around at the now empty streets, I took aim and popped two shots undetected.

The only sounds too follow was the dull thump as my rounds connected with their targets, both of them dropping like a sack of potatoes. I sprinted across the abandoned encampment, grabbed them by their collars, and smashed myself through the door of the hut, accompanied by the scream of Goss's woman as she got off him, covering her bare chest. "Lance, wait!"

I ignored his pleas, popping a round into her head. He covered his face in anguish, moaning unhappily to himself as he stared down at the lifeless figure while blood pooled around the base of the bed. Keeping my sniper trained on him, I pulled his two dead guards in and closed the door behind him as he cried to himself.

"Goss, shut up. You brought this on yourself," I warned.

"She didn't do anything. You coldhearted bastard," he muttered.

"Nor did the seventeen dead people I have lying in my camp," I debated.

He laughed to himself before smashing his hand angrily against the dresser, knowing his time on this earth was over. "Just tell me why ... Why did you do it? All you had to do was let us live our lives and fight the fiends, but you couldn't just live with the fact that I didn't want to be aligned with you," I asked emotionally.

He shrugged. "I am who I am, Lance. You know that. I'll never change. If you're not with me, you're against me. Go ahead. Kill me. Whoever takes my place will be just as bad," he explained.

"That's a risk I'm willing to take," I whispered, shouldering the rifle and shooting a single shot into his chest.

He gasped for air, clutching the wound as he glanced from it to me. I let the rifle fall to my side, letting out a sigh of relief and wanting him to die painfully. He began swearing profanity at me as he rolled out of the bed, convulsing on the floor while blood spewed everywhere.

He crawled across the floor and grabbed a hold of my leg, but I kicked his hand away effortlessly and watched him die in agony. He let out his final breath, and I kicked him over to his side as his eyes glazed over. What little life he was clinging on to evaporated into the cool night's breeze.

As silently as I had come, I exited the camp, sprinted back to the river, followed it to the field, and then plotted a grid on my compass to follow it back to base, the warm feeling of revenge guiding every step. As I arrived back to camp, daybreak was just starting to fight its way through the trees' canopy. I strode across the silent camp's courtyard to where my hut lay peacefully in the corner. All the dead had been buried, and the damaged huts had been repaired.

A few soldiers gave me respectful nods, which I returned. A dull smile was plastered to my face. I knew everything was going to be all right. I carefully opened the door to my hut and chuckled to myself at the sight of Lara, who was snoring peacefully at our table. She had passed out on the window sill, having been waiting for me to get back. My pendant was grasped in her fist. When I gave her a gentle kiss on her forehead, she stirred awake.

"Lance?" she whispered.

I nodded. A smile of joy spread across her face as her bottom lip quivered. I ran my hand along her face and came to a rest on her lip, which stopped quivering as I leaned down and gave her another kiss. She threw her hands around me, making out with me as she giggled in excitement. She reattached the pendant around my neck before returning her attention to making out with me.

She began to strip down, and I did the same. We didn't say anything, because nothing needed to be said. She led me over to the bed, shooting me a sexy look over her shoulder before laying me down and slipping off her underwear as I ran my hand along her body gratefully. Once we had finished, I was greeted by Grant outside as I went to check on the men.

"You going to wipe that silly smirk off your face or just let everyone in the whole camp know you just got laid?" he asked playfully as we exchanged our handshake, happy to see each other again.

"Don't worry, man. We will find you someone," I said with a smirk.

He laughed, waving the offer away. "There is no girl out there who will ever be Ellie," he told me.

I remained silent, reminiscing on the memories of his old girlfriend, who was one of my best friends, growing up in the resistance. "You know," I began, finally breaking the silence. "I felt the same way when Rachel died, and then I met Lara, who reminded me what it was like to live again," I explained to him. "I'm sure Ellie would want you to feel the same way."

He chuckled to himself, laughed in agreement, and gave me a thankful pat on the back. "Thanks, Lance, but when this is all over and my time is up, I'll see her again," he muttered stubbornly.

I returned the pat on his back, accepting his answer as we went to go round up the men for another day of training, knowing the hardest test of the war was yet to come.

CHAPTER 17

Eight years later

Weeks folded into months, and months turned into years. The Revolutionary Force had grown over the years into a true army in the war. Our presence could be felt all around the region as every day passed, forcing the NWO to refocus on the war and the fiends signing a truce between our two factions. We now had nine different camps, spanning a hundred-kilometer radius for our operations.

All that had to be set aside though, as today was a very important day. "You ready to go, bud?" I asked, glancing over at Joshua, who was packing his hunting kit.

"Yes, sir."

I reached over with a smirk and messed up his hair. I grabbed my own kit and stood up, letting the soft morning rays of the summer sun bounce off my face. I couldn't help but watch as the young boy, now fifteen, packed up his kit and shouldered it before joining me by my side. Eight long hard-fought years had passed by, turning the once timid kid into a man before my eyes.

"You boys be safe out there," Lara called from behind us, leaning against the deck of our hut while cradling a freshly brewed coffee.

"We always are," Joshua called back to her before beginning his trek across the camp to his old village.

She sent me a warm smile, blowing a kiss, which I returned along with a reassuring wink. *"You take care of him, Lance,"* she whispered into my head as I turned having to do a light jog over to his side.

"He won't leave my sight," I promised.

"She bugging you in your head?" he asked, glancing over at me as we crested the small hill of our camp and broke into the tree line.

I laughed, holding a tree branch aside for him as he followed. "You know her too well, my boy," was all I could say.

He sighed, but I placed a reassuring hand on his back. "She cares about you, Joshua. We both do."

He nodded, deep in thought as we followed the long, windy path toward his village. That day marked the eighth anniversary since I had saved him from his home after the massacre. It was tradition now to make the long trek every year for him to say his piece to his mother's grave. "Looks like a good spot for a rabbit," he muttered, glancing down at a few individual trails through the mud.

I nodded my agreement, leaning up against a tree. I watched carefully as he grabbed some moss from a small tree for bait and then set up a funnel with sticks and branches, tying snare wire to a sturdy log above a path that seemed to frequently be used by them. "That is very well done," I encouraged him, giving the snare a quick examination.

"Thank you, sir," he muttered, packing up his kit. He

glanced over at me as I stood up, wiped the dirt off my pants, and took a sip of water from my canteen.

"Shall we?" I asked, nodding back to the direction of his village.

He nodded, and we headed back along the trail. He kept glancing over at me. I could tell something was on his mind. "What is it, Joshua?" I finally asked after catching him glance back for the fifth or sixth time.

"Why is it that every other boy my age is allowed to fight but you and Lara refuse to let me contribute to the war?" he asked, clearly frustrated.

"You are contributing to the war. Hunting is a respectable occupation in the resistance. No army has ever won a war on an empty stomach," I debated, taking out a knife to slice a tree as we passed to mark our way back.

He gave me an unhappy sigh, and we paused as he set up another snare. "I want to kill fiends, not rabbits," he muttered with a resentful stare at the trap.

"If something was to happen to you, I would never be able to forgive myself," I finally told him.

"I'm fifteen now, sir. Every other boy gets to choose their occupation at fifteen. I should be able to choose my own path in life as well. You cannot protect me forever."

Folding my arms across my chest, all I could offer was a firm nod, knowing he spoke the truth. As much as I hated to admit it, Joshua reminded me of myself growing up. He was very stubborn, a quick learner, and always put others before himself. I knew he would be a great soldier one day, perhaps even better than myself, but Lara would never allow it.

"We will talk to the boss when we get back," I offered, giving him false hope. I felt the instant guilt from my statement as his face brightened up with the hope of finally being accepted into the resistance.

It only took us another hour and a half before we were overlooking the village, which seemed we had once relied on as a life line not so long ago. Following him down to the ghost town below, I kept my eyes peeled, knowing that the NWO and fiends actively patrolled through this area for supplies and a place to stay. Joshua, unaware of the danger, continued to walk along the side of the road toward the graveyard.

Once we arrived at his mother's grave, I took off my headdress and gave him a respectful nod. I then took my leave to the entrance of the cemetery to give him some time alone.

"Hello, Mother," he began, kneeling down by the grave. He then rummaged around in his backpack, retrieved a freshly picked lily, and set it at the base of the gravestone. "I know it's been awhile since we last spoke, but I'm doing well. Lara and Lance have opened up their arms to me, allowing me into their family. Things are looking up around camp as well. Every day that goes by seems like another victory for the humans. Some of the boys think the war will be over by the end of the year. I'm not that foolish to believe such things. This war will truly never be over, but at least we can always hold on to the hope of peace, I suppose. I've made some new friends around camp. Jessica is doing great as well. I think she's the one."

I glanced over at the kid, a smirk spreading across my face. As Joshua knelt there, his eyes closed, he blushed to himself as he talked about how much he loved Christopher's daughter. He rambled on about a few other things around camp before opening his eyes, placing a kiss on his hand,

and then placing it on the tombstone. "I miss you, Mother. Stay safe up there." He got up and dusted himself off.

"Ready to go, slugger?" I called over to him, throwing my ball cap back on.

He nodded, grabbing his stuff, and we headed back up the way we came. We arrived back to camp just as midday began to set in. "Thanks for everything, Lance," he told me with a hug once we were back in the safety of the camp.

I laughed, giving his back a pat. "No problem, kid. Make sure to bring those rabbits to the kitchen and get them gutted up," I told him, handing the two rabbits slung over my shoulder that he had caught upon retrieving the snares on the way back to camp.

I watched lovingly as he nodded his obedience and headed off to the kitchen. Heading back across the camp, I entered my hut and was greeted by the sight of Lara tidying up the house. She glanced back at me, a smile spreading across her face as she came over. She then grabbed my kit and placed it by the bedside.

"How was that," she asked. She briefly left my side to pour a glass of water, came back, and offered it to me.

I accepted the offer with a thankful kiss before taking a sip, mulling over the day's events to myself. "Well ..." I began. "He's growing quickly."

She giggled to herself, nodding her agreement. "He wants to join the resistance," I muttered, taking another sip. I already knew her answer.

"Absolutely not!" she exclaimed, hitting my arm unhappily with a look of disgust.

"He's a man now, Babe. We rescued him, raised him ... We can't protect him anymore," I debated. "I think it's time for him to make his own decisions."

She shot me an unhappy glare, shooing away the conversation. "How are things going between him and Christopher's daughter?" she asked with a smirk, glancing up from folding a bed sheet.

"You mean Jessica?"

She nodded. "Good. He thinks she's the one," I muttered.

With an understanding nod, she laughed to herself. "I think we're going to need to have the talk with him soon."

I laughed. "Sounds like a not-me job, and I'm busy with this whole winning-the-war thing anyway," I joked.

She laughed, giving me a playful slap on the arm. I glanced out the window as a commotion began outside. There was a crowd gathering around the edge of the camp. "We need a medic over here!" came the cry from one of our main gate's guards.

I dropped what I was doing, and Lara and I raced out the hut over to the front gate where a guard was kneeling over an injured woman. "Move aside, soldier. I got her," Lara instructed, kneeling beside the woman.

My jaw almost dropped to the ground as the mystery woman looked up to Lara, a weak smile spreading across her face. Lara's eyes widened. We stared at the woman as if not believing our eyes.

"Carana?" Lara whispered.

She nodded, the two of them embracing. "We had given up hope!" Lara cried in disbelief, tears springing to her eyes.

Carana chuckled, patting the now sobbing Lara's back. "Rashellia is alive," she whispered.

"You should see her. She's a little lady now. She looks exactly like the two of you," she continued.

I glanced at her hand, which was clutching a gunshot

wound on her stomach. "Quick, help me get her to the medical hut," I called to Grant.

We helped lift her up and escorted her through the now well established camp to our medical clinic where Dr. Lamontain was sitting reading a book. "Quick, get her up on the cot," he instructed.

"She's lost a lot of blood," I told him as Lara began to heal the wounds as well as she could.

"Blood," Carana kept whispering.

I began to unroll my sleeve, but Grant stopped me, undoing his. "I'm not stupid. I know you give yours to Lara. She can have mine," he told me.

I gave him a thankful nod and stepped back as he offered his arm to Carana, who wasted no time and sank her teeth deep into his arm. He winced in pain as I patted his back. "It sucks. I know it does, man. She's almost done." I tried to comfort him.

One she had finished, Lara healed his arm. Carana wiped away the blood from her mouth, giving a thankful smile to him. "This one is cute," she said, glancing over at Lara. The four of us laughed, lightening the mood.

She will be fine. I need everyone to leave now, please. Carana needs her sleep," Dr. Lamontain insisted, cutting our reunion short.

We obediently left, the hut door slamming behind us. Lara jumped for joy, letting out an excited cry as she wrapped me into a hug. "She's alive! … She's alive!" she kept screaming.

I glanced around as others gathered to see the commotion. I gave her a kiss, sharing the excitement. "I told you we would get her back."

"Grant, get Ryan. We need to start planning right away!" I called over to him.

"Sure thing," he called back, taking his leave in search of the others.

I led Lara into the HQ hut, where she happily flopped down. Five or ten minutes past by before Ryan, Christopher, and Grant arrived with maps in hand.

"So as you all know, the target is South Lassetia," I began, unfolding my map in front of them. "It's about a three-day hike from here. We will stage at this point here, about a kilometer away, and hit them at dusk. Grant, how many men do we have?"

"Ninety-three fit for duty," he replied.

"That's perfect. We will leave a small group of thirteen men back here with the women and children. The rest will participate in the attack," I told him.

"When do you think we will be stepping off?" Christopher asked.

I shrugged. "It all depends on Carana's recovery. We still need information about the inside, and the men still need time to prepare," I told him.

He nodded in agreement. "Anything to add?" I asked Ryan, who had been mysteriously quiet through the entire conversation.

"So all this is for the half-blood child?" he asked.

The room went silent as we all stared at him in disbelief. "She's my daughter," I told him.

"I know," he said, holding up his hands peacefully. "It's just we're going to lose a lot of people for your daughter."

"It's for more than just her ... I mean, come on, this is what we've been waiting for, the moment to take down South Lassetia, the fiends' stronghold in this area. Not to mention, there are probably hundreds of prisoners in there for us to free," I told him.

He folded his arms across his chest, not buying it. "And you think we can do all this with eighty men?" he asked.

Lara jumped into the conversation, saving me, her voice filled with emotion. "Ryan, we've known each other eight and a half years now, so you know I would not lie to you when I say that Rashellia is more than just our daughter, more even than a half-blood. She is the key to winning the war. When she comes of age, her powers will be beyond imagination. Once that day arrives, the fiends will harness it, and all hope will be lost for mankind. This mission is more than a rescue mission for our daughter; it is to preserve the future of your children. Our actions from here on out will be read in the history books by your grandchildren and your grandchildren's great-grandchildren. That is what you can tell your men."

She angrily got up and stormed out of the hut, not awaiting a reply. "I'm sorry, Lance," he muttered, staring at the ground in shame.

"It's fine," I told him, waving his apology away. "Your question is justified, and it will be what many of those fighting for us will ask as well. If we are successful, we could change the tide of the war."

"And if we're not?" Grant asked.

"Well, I won't be alive to find that out. The only way I'm leaving there is with my daughter," I promised him. They all remained silent, so I dismissed them with a nod, getting up and heading outside to attend to Lara.

I did not have to search long. She was at our usual mountain cliff, the wind playing with her hair as she fiddled with a stick; she was staring out at the vast ocean, deep in thought.

"You okay?" I whispered, taking a seat beside her.

She glanced over with a faint smile, nodding before her gaze returned to the ocean. "I just feel so lost without her. These eight years have felt like an eternity. I've tried my best not to let it affect me, and to hide it from you and Joshua, but now that it's finally happening, I can't hide it anymore." Her voice quivered as she took a big breath and then let it out.

"I know," was all I could say in my best attempt to comfort her.

"I need to speak to Carana," she insisted, chucking the stick off the cliff.

"We will tonight, all right?" I asked.

"Deal," she whispered.

The buzz of excitement from our new arrival was ripe in the air when Lara and I returned back to camp. Everyone was giving us happy looks; some came up and congratulated us, while others talked among themselves about the upcoming battle for South Lassetia. If there was ever a time to do it, it was now. Our army had never been stronger; it was the middle of summer, so we wouldn't have to battle the elements; and morale in the camp had never been as high as it had been for the past few weeks.

Lara and I sat anxiously outside the medical hut for hours on end. It had begun to get dark when finally the door creaked open, revealing Doctor Lamontain. "She's ready for you," he announced, waving us in.

Laying eyes on Carana for the first time in eight years was a lot to take in. It was clear that the lab had changed her; she looked a lot more worn as she mustered what little strength she could to pull herself upright in bed. "Looking good," I joked as Lara and I took a seat by her side.

Lara gave me a playful punch; I made a show of mock

pain, clutching my arm, and got a laugh out of Carana. "I've seen better days," she told us.

We nodded our sympathy. "Thank you for all you've done for us," I told her.

She smiled, giving me a nod. "It wasn't just for you. David has lost his life for her, and I couldn't let his death be in vain," she reminded us.

"He was a good man," was all I could say as fond memories of our old friend flashed through my mind.

"We will never forget him and Tina for what they did to try and save Rashellia," Lara added.

"Well, I suppose I should fill you in on the last eight years, huh?" Carana asked with a smirk, we all laughed.

She sat back in the bed before continuing. "Once I had left camp, after you were shot, I wandered around for days, finally bumping into a fiend patrol. My story was that I had been separated from my unit, and surprisingly enough, they bought it. They were wary at first of letting me interact with what they call their subjects, but after about two years of my working there, they decided to give me a shot at an internship with what they called their 'special project.'"

"Rashellia?" Lara whispered.

Carana nodded. "She was only four years old, but she was already walking and talking like a child twice her age; they said she had superhuman intelligence."

"She probably got that from me," I interrupted.

They laughed before Carana took a sip of water and continued with her story: "Rashellia instantly took a liking to me, and we forged a relationship through the next six years. She is a beautiful little girl, and as she grew, I could see both of your traits growing within her."

"What about her powers?" Lara asked.

"Those are developing as well," she added, taking another sip of water as her expression darkened, as if finding a memory which she would rather have forgotten. "She does not know how to tap into her power yet though. It would be driven only by anger; she has killed three guards already. They moved her to a high-security vault where she spends most of her days without company, which only adds to the fire within her."

I cringed at the thought of my daughter being locked in a dark room all day, every day, for the rest of her life, being turned into some sideshow for the fiends. All I knew was that we had to get her out of there. "You know the inside?" I asked.

She smirked. "Like the back of my hand."

"Good. You rest up; we're going to have a long journey ahead of us," I told her, giving her a pat on the leg as I got up to leave.

"Where are you going?" Lara asked.

"I need to speak with Fiona,"

She nodded, letting me go. I retrieved the shell from our hut, made the journey down to the sea's edge, and placed the shell in the water before giving it three hard blows. I waited; nothing happened. An hour passed, and still nothing. Then just as I was ready to give up hope, the familiar voice of Fiona came from the wake of the sea: "You have summoned me, Lance?"

I nodded, glancing up from the ground at the mythical creature wading her way through the surf to greet me at the land. "It's Rashellia," I said. "She's still alive."

Fiona nodded. "Of course she is. The fiends would never let their prize possession perish." Then she added nonchalantly, "My men have reported increased fiend patrols from the sky around every major river in the area. My guess is that they have reason to be concerned?"

"Our spy has escaped from the prison," I informed her. "She knows everything. In a week's time we are going to assault Lassetia and save Rashellia."

"Are you sure that is a good idea, Lance? All it takes is for one fiend patrol to spot you, and they will move her, never to be seen again," she told me.

"Let me worry about that, Fiona. Are your men ready to fight?" I asked her.

"Of course," came her reply.

"Then let them know there is a river not far from our camp that connects to the ocean. Meet us up there with your men in one week's time," I ordered.

She nodded. "I hope for your sake and Lara's that you are not making a mistake, Lance." She then got up, brushing herself off, and vanished back into the wake, leaving behind no trace of our visit.

Training started immediately the following day. We had physical-fitness sessions three times a day. There was target practice, and we brushed every one up on their individual patrolling skills. By the time the next week rolled around, I knew we were ready.

Early the next day, under the cover of the morning mist, I made my way to a river not far from camp where Fiona and fifteen Shellians were waiting.

"This is it?!" I asked her.

"They are hand-selected, Lance. You are looking at the best soldiers the Atlantic army has to offer," she assured me.

I nodded my gratitude. "This river should lead all the way to South Lassetia's front door. There is a moat that surrounds the laboratory. After you guys have recced the position, report back to me at this position," I told her, pointing to where our location would be on the map. "During the assault, I will need you and your men to clear the staging area at the main gate in order for us to set up and assault the interior of the place."

She nodded, giving my hand a firm shake—her cold, slimy feel still unfamiliar to my hand. "Good luck, Lance."

"You too, Fiona."

Without another word said, she and her men vanished into the river. I raised myself up off my knee, taking in the beauty of our camp's surroundings one last time. It felt as though the music of the waking forest serenaded my walk back to camp.

As I reached the edge of the camp, a rustling in the bushes behind me caught my attention. I stopped, and it stopped as well.

"Whoever you are, come on out," I finally called, turning to identify the culprit as Joshua emerged from the cover of the tree line.

"You're going after her, aren't you?" he whispered.

I nodded and took a seat on a log overlooking camp, patting a spot by my side. Silently, he came over and joined me on the log. "You will be killed," he said.

I glanced over at the teenager, who was staring gloomily at the ground while fiddling with a stick in the dirt. "Probably," I whispered, placing a reassuring hand on his back. "Everyone must die eventually though, Joshua."

His lip quivered as he remained silent, sharing a moment with me as we watched the camp below coming to life. "I'm going with you," he finally said.

I glanced over at him, and our eyes met. I could see the passionate fire burning in his eyes, but I was quick to douse it with a shake of my head. "I need you to stay back with the others to protect the camp."

"But—" he began to protest.

I held up my hand, silencing him. "You're special, Joshua; I knew that the first day I laid my eyes on you. When I'm gone, people will need someone to follow, a person to believe in. You are that person, Joshua. You will lead our people to peace and win this war."

He shook his head, but I sent him a reassuring smile, lifting my hand to run it along the faint scar across his cheek. "Rashellia will need your help. There is an evil inside all of us, and you must help her find the right path. Teach her right from wrong, good from evil. Can I count on you?" I asked him.

He nodded, and I unslung my Timberwolf, took off my mag, and cocked back the action to make the chambered round fall harmlessly to the ground. Taking the round, I brushed the dirt off it, reloading it into the magazine and then handing the unloaded weapon to him as he stared at me questioningly. "I want you to have this, Joshua," I began. "It belonged to my father many years ago."

"Tha … Thank you, sir," he stammered, looking the weapon over in disbelief.

I gave him a gentle pat on his back, we got up, and I gave him a hug. "You're a good kid, Joshua; I'm counting on you to finish what I've started," I told him.

He smirked, saying, "I'll do my best, sir."

Lara was waiting outside our hut when I showed up. She gave me a kiss and a questioning stare. "We are set?" she asked.

I nodded. "The Shellians are on their way to South Lassetia as we speak."

"There is no going back now," she whispered.

It took about two hours to round up the rest of the men, but finally we were ready to go. Grant and I led the way. The going was rough with none of the terrain wanting to cooperate. "Who put all these hills here?" Grant joked as we stopped for a break.

We set off again, making very little progress; that day we traveled only two or three kilometers. But it was better than nothing. We came to a halt at Sambro Lake, setting up camp for the night there. "I want light discipline, no fires, and two roving patrols," I told Grant. "Also," I said, pointing to a spot on the map, "I would like an outpost set up here for early detection."

He obediently nodded and then left to fulfill his orders. Lara chuckled to herself. I glanced over at her questioningly. "What's so funny?"

She waved my question away, giggling to herself. "'I want this, I want that.' Grr, big old mean Lance laying down the law!" she joked.

With a laugh, I gave her a playful punch on the shoulder. "I have to assert my dominance; otherwise the men would not listen," I explained to her.

"I know," she replied, placing a reassuring kiss on my cheek.

"It's just funny to see how you've changed since when we first met—a shy young boy too scared to even look at naked women."

I laughed. "What I'd give to be young again!"

Luckily for us, the terrain and weather cooperated for the next three days, allowing our journey to South Lassetia to progress without any major problems. There were a few sprained ankles and such injuries where men were sent back to base, but we still had more than enough for our attack. At length, we arrived at our destination.

Grant, Lara, Carana, and I lay in the brush surrounding the laboratory, staring at it quietly as enemy patrols roamed around the perimeter of the complex outside.

"Here it is," Grant muttered, staring out motionlessly at the building in front of us.

"Yes, seven inches of concrete separating me and my daughter," I told him.

"It's going to be a bitch to gain entry into this place," he said.

"The south side is their weakest," Carana informed us.

"What side is this?" Grant whispered back.

"The south side," she said.

Grant let out an unamused grunt, taking his eyes off the complex to shoot Carana a smirk. "You know, Carana, over the eight years we've been apart, I've really missed your sense of humor," he joked.

Carana smirked, returning the stare. "Me, not so much."

"Cut it out," I whispered.

The four of us observed the position for another fifteen to twenty minutes and then snuck back to our patrol base, where the others were anxiously waiting.

"Sir, there is a Shellian by the name of Fiona waiting for you," a young recruit informed me as we arrived back to our position.

"Excellent; bring her over here," I told him as the four of us took a knee in the dirt, laying the map out in front of us. Ryan, Fiona, and Christopher showed up a minute or two later and took a seat beside us.

"You've seen the place?" I asked Fiona.

She nodded, so I continued, "Okay, so the plan is that

my men will attack from the south side. I'm sending five men over to the north side where your men will start the attack off in order to divert the fiends' attention. Once they are focused on the north side, I need you and a few others to swim over to the south side; there are four or five armed guards that guard the bridge. They need to be eliminated and the gate unlocked so we can gain entry."

"Be careful," Grant added. "There is some sort of electric force field surrounding it; I saw a bird find that out the hard way this morning. I would assume there is a way to deactivate it from the guard shack."

"Okay, we will do our best. Is there anything else?" Fiona asked.

"Yes," I said, glancing over at Carana. "What side is Rashellia being held on? Northwest? Okay. Then Fiona, I will need your men to shift there for our extraction once we reach her. The plan is to blow a hole through the roof and repel down to the parking lot below. We will then make the fifty-meter sprint to the water's edge, where your men can extract us safely out of harm's way."

"We will be there," she promised.

We concluded the meeting, and everyone dispersed to go tell the others of the plan. Grant stayed behind, lighting his last cigarette and taking a puff before handing it to me.

"Just like old times, eh?" he muttered.

"There's a lot more at stake now," I replied.

He muttered his agreement. "Grant ..." I paused to make sure my next sentence was as clear as possible. "If something is to happen to me tomorrow ... You leave me there, okay? I'm not leaving without Rashellia. Make sure Lara and the others are brought back safely. The revolutionary force is yours if I'm to die ... okay? Promise me—please."

CHAPTER 18

I found myself lying belly-down in the grass, staring out at South Lassetia with my men the next morning. My stomach felt like it was doing cartwheels as I glanced at my watch and then returned my attention to the complex. Not a sound could be heard but the peaceful chirping of the birds.

As I took another look at my watch, my grip tightened around the assault rifle in my hands, and I whispered "Thirty seconds" to my men. The message rushed down to either end of the line. I could feel myself shaking but had to put the fear aside—not for me, not for my men, but for Rashellia. Everything we had worked for had come down to this one moment.

The sounds of machine gun fire shattered the stillness, making me flinch. The assault had started. Jumping to my feet, I yelled at the top of my lungs, motivating the men to attack. "Come on, let's go kill these sons of bitches," I kept yelling, as everyone screamed their war cries, sprinting toward the bridge.

The whizzing sounds of gunfire began to sound all around us as men fell victim to the return fire, dropping like flies. "Keep going; don't stop!" I yelled over the din of war.

Huffing and puffing, I narrowly avoided a rocket that exploded fifteen meters to my right. Mortars began to rain around us, but it was too late for the fiends. Joy overtook me as Fiona and a few other Shellians emerged from over the sides of the bridge, slicing the fiends' throats before they even knew they were there.

Fiona ran into the guard hut. There was a loud grinding noise as the force field was deactivated and the gate swung open. We filled into the bridge, finding refuge under the building.

"Grant!" I yelled over the hissing of gunfire. He came running to my side, and I pointed to the window. "Crossbow ready with the hook."

He nodded, taking a step out from the building and firing into it. It was a direct hit as he pulled it firm, tying the bow to a piece of the bridge.

"Get demolition up there!" I yelled, pointing to the metal jail bars protecting the window from outsiders.

A young private shimmied his way up the rope, attaching the c4 explosives to the window. His eyes widened, and I cringed as an assault rifle opened up on him from inside. His body came smashing down, landing in front of us, dead as a rock.

Fumbling for a grenade, I cursed under my breath, pulled the pin, and chucked it up through the window. I was rewarded by the fearful cry of a fiend.

The explosion rocked the ground around us. I searched the young boy's body and found his detonator in his pocket. "C4!" I yelled, everyone covered their ears, and I clicked the detonator together, causing an explosion twice as large as the grenade.

The metal bars protecting the window went flying, allowing our entry.

"Ryan!" I yelled. There was no response. "Ryan!" I yelled again.

"He's dead, sir," someone called back.

"Take these men around to the northwest side," I shouted at the man who had spoken up. I couldn't take time now to mourn Ryan's death.

Lara, Grant, Carana, Christopher, and I then climbed the rope, entering the building. A guard poked his head into the room. We killed him before he even knew what hit him.

Racing into the hall, we could see that things were in chaos as alarms blared and the walls flashed with red emergency lights. Carana ran over to a billboard that had a map of the building. "This way! We need to reach her before they put her in a safe-holding cell!" she shouted.

We raced down the hall, turning corner after corner in a maze of hallways. When we reached a large metal door resembling a bank vault, I knew we had made it. There was a shot that rang out behind us. Christopher groaned, clutching his stomach, turning, and killing the soldier that had discovered us. "Chris!" Lara yelled. It was too late though.

He clutched the wound, slumping to the ground. "Get her. I'll cover," he coughed through a mouthful of blood, fighting to stay conscious.

I knelt down and grabbed his hand. Our eyes met. "Thank you, man." He nodded, raising his weapon. I turned to see him kill a lab assistant that had unknowingly raced around the corner straight into us. "Take care of my daughter," he begged.

"We will," I promised.

"Shit," Carana muttered, staring at the door.

"What?" I asked, glancing up at her.

"They've completely redone the security to her room."

She glanced over at the dead lab assistant, an idea dawning on her face. Running over to the body, she dragged the man over to the security system, placing his hand on a blue pad and swiping his card. An automated voice said something in Jural, and Carana held the man's head up and opened his eyes toward the screen.

Lasers came out and scanned his face; then the machine said something else.

The door opened and revealed a little girl. The moment I set eyes on her, I knew it was our daughter. She had every characteristic her mother and I carried.

"Auntie 159!" the young girl yelled joyfully, running over to Carana as we entered the large white experiment room.

Lara and I stared at her in disbelief as she ran by, giving Carana a hug. "You did it! You came back for me!" she cried out.

Tears sprang to Lara's eyes as we watched the girl, and for that one instant, time seemed to freeze. Nothing mattered—the war, trying to survive day by day on little to no food or water, not even escaping this hellhole. All that mattered was our daughter. "She's beautiful," I whispered, giving Lara's head a kiss.

She whimpered her agreement, returning the kiss. Carana glanced up, a smile on her face. "Rashellia, I would like you to meet your parents."

The young girl turned, her eyes widening in disbelief. "Mom? Dad?" unable to hold the tears of joy back any longer Lara and I kneeled down to embrace the child.

"I knew you would save me!" Rashellia cried into our arms. "I knew there was more than this place!"

I smiled, unfastening the heart-shaped pendant around my neck and handing it to Rashellia.

"It's beautiful," she whispered.

I nodded and opened the locket so she could see her family. "This is your two aunts and your grandmother," I whispered back.

"Tina and Kate?" she asked.

"Yes," I replied.

"All dead?"

I nodded. "You met Tina when you were just a baby," I told her.

She nodded, staring back down at the locket. "Carana told me the story; she gave her life to try to save me?"

I nodded and motioned toward Grant. "We all have worked so hard for this day," I told her.

She nodded her gratitude. "Thank you, Dad. I will never forget this."

"We should go," Grant urged.

I nodded in agreement, pulling myself together. Grant tossed sticky C-4 up at the ceiling while we all cowered in the corner hugging each other for protection. "Firing!" he shouted.

The room instantly filled with smoke as the building trembled from the explosion. Coughing and sputtering, Grant tossed a rope out the man-size hole and secured it. "Here," I told him, handing him my weapon so it wouldn't get in the way. He shouldered it, climbed up through the hole, reached down, and held out his hand. "Next!" he called.

I gave Lara a boost; she was next so that then she and Grant could help pull Rashellia out from above. Next I lifted Rashellia with the help of Carana, holding her up to the two already out. "Reach, Honey!" I whispered urgently.

Two shots rang out, and Carana's neck exploded, spraying purplish fiend blood all over me as I screamed in pain, the three of us crumpling to the ground. I clutched my stomach in agony as I rolled over and faced six armed guards led by a scientist who was chuckling to himself. "You must be Lance."

Sucking in a painful breath of air, I stared in sorrow at Carana. She was dead, her eyes glazed over, probably killed before she hit the ground. I felt myself fading as Rashellia began screaming.

"Daddy ... Daddy? Are you okay?" she kept sobbing, hugging me close.

I could hear Lara from above us, yelling, "We have to save them!" She kept screaming, but it seemed that Grant had held true to his promise as her cries became more and more distant.

I let out a sigh of relief, knowing this was the end, there was no way of escape, no chance of a miraculous revival. This was the end of the line, and as weird as it was to think it, I was completely at peace with that thought. I hugged Rashellia close, giving her a kiss as I groaned, sat up, and patted her hair back. "Daddy has to go, Hun. I love you, I always will," I told her, trying to control my quivering voice.

She began to sob uncontrollably with her head resting against my chest. "I love you, Dad! I don't want you to go."

I gave her a pat, looking up at the others in defeat. The scientist gave me a nod, allowing me to say my goodbyes. "I'm not going anywhere; I'll always be right here," I whispered, patting her chest.

She sniffed, wiping away a tear and patting her own chest. "I'll never forget you, Dad."

I glanced up at the man in charge. "You have what you want, Sir; let my friends go," I pleaded.

He remained silent for a second, and then a sneer crossed his face as he brought a radio to his mouth and ordered something in Jural. "As you wish," he replied. "I need to send a clear message to your rebel counterparts anyway."

"Lance?" A weak gurgle came from behind us.

I turned to see Christopher lying on his side, assault rifle aimed at the crowd.

"Down!" I shouted, grabbing Rashellia and wrapping her in a hug to protect her.

He never got to fire a shot though. As the fiends lit him up, Christopher lifelessly dropped the weapon. "No!" Rashellia screamed.

Two guards came, one tearing me from her as the other held her back. As I was ripped away, I saw her devastating power. It was something scary, something the world would one day see. She let out a scream and grabbed the guard with a ferocious growl. He erupted in flames, disintegrating within seconds into thin air. She ran toward me, but it was too late; the door slammed shut, leaving nothing but her banging and wails of despair as the entire room lit up into a blinding inferno. The solid steel door closed, leaving us in silence as the sound of her cries was extinguished.

The scientist smoothed his coat, glancing over at me

as more armed guards joined us. "Let's get on with this, shall we?"

They escorted me to the rooftop, placing me on the edge overlooking the world below. I took a deep breath and closed my eyes to feel the light breeze the day had to offer. The sounds of guns cocking filled the air around me, and I let out my final breath.

No fear, no anger, no sadness—just accepting my fate.

"Any last words?" the scientist asked.

I laughed to myself, glancing back over my shoulder at him. "You will never conquer her."

A single shot rang out, ending my life.

The scientist peered over the ledge as Lance's body hit the cement bridge below, a satisfied expression spread across his face as he watched the retreat of the leaderless rebels back into the Harush Forest. "Pitiful," he whispered to himself, gloating in his victory. He turned heading back into the building. He would not have been smiling, however, had he known that this one miniscule act of war would one day pave the way to the freedom of the entire human race.

Printed in the United States
By Bookmasters